GETTING OFF ON THE WRONG FOOT

(AND OTHER TALES OF MALE TICKLE
TORTURE, DEVIOUS EDGING, AND
FORCED FOOT WORSHIP)

by James T. Medak

NOTE: Under no circumstances should you read this book while wearing shoes, socks, or sandals.

Table of Contents

This book is dedicated to the memory of Jay Grafmiller

Let me be honest with you dear reader: I honestly thought I would never, ever, ever write a third book, but not for the reasons that you think.

Part of being a writer of erotica means that I'm also very much a consumer of it: I've read countless male tickle and foot fetish tales, and as wonderful as they often are, I wind up running into the same problems: the tropes, the scenarios, and the outcomes are almost always the same. Sometimes it's the very way in which the acts carried out within are described that make or break a story, as I'd much rather read a sentence like "the feather dragged over his nipple, causing the top to lightly harden" than something like "HAHAHAHEEHEEA" or what have you. In short, when I started down this journey of crafting top-notch jackoff literature (at least top notch in my own deluded mind), I had one abiding rule: I never wanted to write the same thing twice. Part of the reason why I've been able to hold to that simple motto is because I only write when I'm absolutely motivated to, which usually means that I've thought or something really, really hot (and for the record, there are times where I've started stories when the inspiration wasn't there, and there's very much a reason why they remain unfinished).

So part of the reason why I'm still amazed you're holding my third book in your hands is because apparently there were new types of stories worth exploring. What I've learned (and loved) about fetishes is that over time, they evolve. The heroes (or victims, depending on your perspective) of my first book were all collegiate types: frat boys and nebbish hipsters, all discovering new contours of their sexuality, often against their will. With this book, all the characters are grown up now, in their mid 20s, living on their own, working full-time jobs, still going to rock concerts and smoking the occasional joint. Their freedom is boundless, their energy almost limitless, and they are still very much in their sexual prime (and let's not forget how goddamn sexy their feet look, plodding around on the hardwood floors of their discount studio apartments in the city).

Aside from the age range of my stories, my actual fetishes have evolved as well. Yes, I still do love a good healthy amount of tickling from a guy at his most helpless, and my obsession over male feet has probably only gotten deeper at times (up to the point where I've coined the term "poppin' a footboner" to describe what it's like when you saw that absolutely perfect pair walk by you -- and yes, it has happened more than once), but one area of increasing interest has been my out-and-out love of everything related to edging. Tying a guy down, dragging a feather across his erect shaft, bringing him closer and closer towards glorious, forced inevitability -- it's nothing short of a rush. I've gotten more and more adept at it over the years, and it's now become a point of great interest and intrigue for me, something which you see more and more of in this book and hopefully in stories to come as well.

Indulge me, if you will, in something sexy thank yous. Enough kind words can't be said about Devan, one of my dear friends and most ardent supporters; the wonderful Joey, who is also a never-ending fountain of encouragement; all the 'Fest and Frat friends including Chad and Roman (both whom, I should mention, are extremely ticklish); incredible industry leaders like Cat from MyFriendsFeet, Ian Marshall, TiedFeetGuy himself, and the wonderful authors Wayne Courtois and Christopher Trevor (whose books you should definitely read) who have shown me nothing but kindness even as I'm just the new kid on the scene. Big props to Michael Kaluzny and the straight guy only known as "Will" for their generous contribution to the cover of this book as well (both will be very handsomely rewarded). Oh, and where would a guy be without the most loving husband a guy could ever ask for? To decades of fun ahead of us, Bas ...

One more special shout-out. Those who know me know full well that even though I come up with devious, delightful, and often terrifically scenarios for these books (and more and more, real life), I'm not always good about characters, often haphazardly basing characters on real-life friends and co-workers outright. Some of them know they have roles in my books, most of them don't, and to all of them, let me say: thank you. I am blessed to have some absolutely amazing friends who serve as amazing inspiration -- friends who not only actively buy my books and read them (despite being straight as hell), but friends who aren't completely weirded out when they find out they have been inserted into a nationally-published book of erotica. To all of them, again, thank you for being who you are (and for that particular one who has appeared in multiple stories in my bibliography, an incredible double-thank to you being so cool about it -- figure I owe you a footrub or something ...).

Now please, dear reader, put your feet up: it's not like you're going anywhere for awhile. In fact, you're not going to be going anywhere for a very, very, very long time ...

--James T. Medak
January 2013

THE GALLERY

+ + +

What's better than obsessing over male feet? Why, obsessing over <u>forbidden</u> male feet of course. Over time, I've gradually learned that I have a very particular "type" of guy that I'm sexually intrigued by (and as I grow older, it changes slightly, like an aging wine ... kinda). Are they in their 20s, vaguely hipster-esque, and have a great deal of facial hair? Well then my goodness, I think I'm set for the evening. Ryan, here, was a co-worker at my former job, and he fit all of those traits to a T. In fact, he actually kind of reminded me of the lead victim of "My Ticklish Revenge" from How to Be a Tickle Slave *the day I met him, so I knew we'd get along famously. I have fantasized and obsessed over his feet and toes for some time, although never got the change to see them (at least until we became Facebook friends -- yes, I'm totally evil), and in lieu of gathering such sweet podiacal eye candy in person, I figured the next best thing would be to write a story about it, and with "The Gallery", I captured exactly what I wanted to do to this sweet boy, and boy did I have a fantastic time writing it.*

Jonathan returned from the restroom, drying his hands on his jeans as he walked, and looked back at the computer where his friend Ryan was sitting. Ryan, a thin guy with penchant for plaid short-sleeve button-down shirts to go with his thin pencil frame, wasn't turning around to acknowledge his approach, though. As the rugged twenty-something Jonathan pulled forward, he saw an image on the screen. A private image. A horribly, horribly private image buried deep in his hard drive that Ryan had discovered. As Jonathan drew closer, his sense of embarrassment and personal horror grew and grew.

There, on the screen, wasn't just a picture of Ryan's bare soles, no. It was far worse: it was a collage. A series of digital photos taken of Ryan's feet in various state of dress: sock-footed, donning flip-flops, his toes peaking out from the covers of Jonathan's futon during one of the drunken nights he must've passed out at Jonathan's place -- a whole litany of foot fetish glory. The collage, however, didn't end with multiple images of Ryan's feet digitally duplicated and splayed out in a quasi-creative fashion, no. In the middle of this art, there were big printed letters saying "You like these feet, don't you? Go ahead and tickle them ...", as if taunting the person who made it. This was 100% genuine jackoff material, and, assuredly, something Ryan wasn't supposed to see.

Once Jonathan was standing next to the computer -- where the friends had been watching stupid YouTube videos earlier -- Ryan turned around, his look of horror complementing Jonathan's blushing face quite well. While Jonathan wanted to call out his friend out for digging through his private picture folders on his computer, he kind of knew that Ryan had the upper hand no matter what.

"What the fuck is this, man?!" shouted Ryan, angry and mortified all at once.

"Dúde," started Jonathan, "let me explain ..."

Ryan stood up. "What's there to explain man? I know you've had a male foot fetish -- that's fine, I don't care about that -- but you've been taking pictures of my feet when I wasn't looking? When I was sleeping here? And you've been jacking off to them? Holy shit dude, this is getting into, like, tuber-creepy territory ..."

"Ryan, I ..."

"Did you do anything to my feet while I was sleeping?"

"No!", exclaimed Jonathan, defiant.

"Did you want to?"

A painful pause filled the air. Jonathan stuttered a bit: "I ... I mean, I'd want to, but there are certain lines between friends that shouldn't ..."

"Jesus Christ, man!" Ryan was angry now, still walking around with his faux-leather almost-work-friendly sports shoes on. "I mean ... god. This is just too weird. I'm too freaked out man, I ... I just can't be around you right now."

"Ryan, don't go ..."

"Did you send those pictures around to anyone?"

"No!" exclaimed Jonathan, again. Jonathan really meant it, too, as he would never do something as tuber-creepy as sharing those photos online with others. They were for his own personal use, and that's it -- not like it justified his actions, of course.

"Why do I get the sense that you're lying?" Ryan was really twisting the knife in at this point.

"Ryan, I'm not lying. I never shared those pictures with anyone?"

"Well I feel humiliated ... and, and kind of terrified."

"Ryan, I understand that. I really do. If you'd just let me ..."

"And your ultimate goal is to tickle them? Tickling my feet would get you horny and get you off? Is that right?"

Jonathan stuttered again, "It's ... you just got to give me a second to ..."

Ryan grabbed his gray hoodie and began heading from the door of his friend's apartment. "You know what? I can't stand this. You went too far, man. Seriously, this is ... sick. I'm telling everyone we know. Yeah. Yeah, that'll show ya!" Ryan was delirious with anger at this point. "Now let me get out of here."

Ryan unlocked the apartment door and left without saying anything else. Jonathan tried to run after him and plead for his return ... but it was pointless. If Ryan really did do what he was going to say, then yeah, he'd be ruined. The two friends went to the same high school. They work at the same place now that they both have Bachelor's degrees. There is, in short, a lot of fallout that could happen from this, and Jonathan, in a word, would be screwed.

The next 30 minutes had Jonathan pacing around his apartment frantically, his hand trembling with nervous tension. All he did was go use the restroom as he usually does. What made Ryan decide to start snooping around on his computer, much less find a folder that far buried in his hard drive? Nothing was making any sense right now. Jonathan wondered if he should call Ryan or text him or ... no. He was pissed off and there was nothing that was going to change his mind, and if there's anything that Jonathan knew, it was that it took a *lot* to piss off Ryan.

Jonathan really didn't want to do it. He didn't want to open up that can of worms, but, really, in a case like this, he had no choice. He picked up his cell phone, and called a number he's called many times before, but this time with a sense of urgency he's never had. A voice on the other end picked up, and Jonathan began to speak: "Hey ... I got a crisis situation here. I ... yep. Ryan, the one I've told you about. I know it'd be a last-minute addition to ... I know. It ... oh trust me, he'll win it. Easy. I'd be more than happy to bet on that but right now I just need some containment. I ... OK, yes, let me give you his address ..."

+ + +

Ryan was sitting on his bed, barefoot. Although his TV was on (turned to one of those "World's Scariest Police Chases" shows, with the volume way down), Ryan wasn't paying attention to it. He was focusing on his feet, and trying to figure out what about them made them appear "sexy" to his now-former friend. He didn't get it: his size 11s were thin, his toes were long, his arches were pretty well curved, and his skin was pasty-white (except on the base of the toes and the heel, as those were a shade red due to constant contact with his shoes/the ground) -- how is that sexually appealing? Here he was, 26 years old, living with his parents still, albeit with a hot girlfriend and now dealing with the fact that his best friend had been taking pictures of his exposed feet for what may very well have been years on end. It was a strange conundrum, and he didn't really want to think about it anymore. He still felt very violated by what he saw on Jonathan's computer. He'd known for years about Jonathan's foot fetish, but he just never thought his own toes would factor into the equation. This still made Ryan feel angry and exposed, and he was about to expose his friend in return. He put his dark gray socks back on and headed for his computer to start posting some stuff on the interwebs when he couldn't help but notice a flashing blue light on the evening street below. Ryan stuck his head out the window and saw a police car pulling up ... to the front of his house.

After a few minutes of those red and blue lights jutting in to his room, sockwalked down to the front door to see what it was all about. His mother stood at the open door speaking to two police officers.

"What's going on, mom?"

She turned to her son with a look of worry on her face. The two officers' faces were practically expressionless.

"Oh honey, it looks like someone may have gone missing and the last place they were seen was at work. The officers here are wondering if you wouldn't mind coming down to the station to view some footage and see if you can't help find this per-- I'm sorry, am I speaking out of turn, officers?"

"No ma'am. You're doing a fine job," said the taller, slightly older one.

"Listen," started Ryan, "I don't really think that ..."

"It'll just be for an hour or so sir. Put some shoes on please and come with us."

Ryan was a bit flabbergasted by the suddenness of this whole thing, and was about to protest, but saw the look on his mom's face -- that look that implied he might be the key to this whole thing -- and couldn't say no. "I'll be right back," he told the officers, grabbing those shoes once more.

The officers were using a standard police car, with a fenced partition between the front and the back seats of the car. When Ryan got in the back with those same work shoes slipped on, the other officer -- shorter, stockier, ethnic but in a way that Ryan couldn't immediately identify -- got in the back with him. Ryan thought this was unusual for sure but didn't say anything of it. The car slowly drove away into the nighttime streets.

The shorter officer sitting next to Ryan began to speak to him while appearing to reach for something under the passenger seat in front of him.

"We thank you for your cooperation, sir. We'll have you home in a few hours."

"I thought you said one hour."

"There's been a change of plans."

"But, we just barely ..."

And in a lightning-fast motion, the officer took a chloroformed rag and placed it right over Ryan's mouth. Before Ryan's brain even comprehended what was going on, it was too late: this too-strong sensation took over his brain, his eyelids seemed to get extremely heavy all of a sudden, and just like that, he plunged into a deep unconscious sleep. All was black.

+ + +

Ryan awoke, groggy. He felt like he was awaking from a sleep so deep that everything felt very dreamlike, surreal, slow motion-y. A strange blue hue of light was penetrating his vision, and everything was all fuzzy. He tried rubbing his eyes ... but couldn't. His arms were stretched out to either side of him, but they were strapped down. Not very hard, mind you, but still within some of those big leather straps that he's seen in insane asylums in films, making sure no harm came to him no matter how hard he struggled. Ryan was still laying down, comfortably, but his arms just wouldn't go. He cussed out loud, but it was to no effect. He stared up and that glowing hue above him, and discovered that, in fact, there were a series of TV monitors positioned directly above him. Each monitor seemed to be tapped into some sort of CCTV, and he was looking at a ... gallery, of some sort. Everything was in black and white, but it looked like a series of hallways painted red. One monitor seemed to be zoomed in on something unusually specific: a piece of smooshed gum. Well, wait, maybe it was ... yeah, smooshed gum on the sole of a shoe. There was a matching shoe right next to it. Well that's weird. Ryan tried propping himself up to get a better view, but ... his legs were also bound. Ryan looked down at this feet and couldn't even see them. Although he was tied down in some sort of room where he couldn't move his arms, his feet seemed to be not just in a set of stocks: they were stuck inside a gigantic black wall. Ryan couldn't see anything outside of the glow of the overhead monitors, but his feet were inside a wall, in another room! It was weird: his feet were in one room and his body was in another. He tried finding something he could anchor his left foot on so that he could maybe get some leverage ... and then his mouth dropped in horror.

He twitched his left foot. The gum-stained foot on the monitor above him moved. He turned his right foot to the side as much as he could, and the right shoe on the monitor did the same. Holy shit: a camera was pointed directly at his feet, which were in another room altogether. He moved his feet up and down as much as he could and looked at the gallery monitor, and ... there he was. His feet were sticking out of a wall at about chest-level, and they were apparently a part of some ... gallery? He looked closely at the monitors and saw that, in fact, there were several other pairs of feet sticking out of the wall, all belonging to guys that were probably just as helpless as he was. Ryan had a bit of a panic moment: this wasn't right. This was ... insane. HE WAS A PIECE OF ART ON DISPLAY AT A GODDAMN FETISH GALLERY. Ryan spent the next 10 minutes screaming at the top of his lungs and struggling as much as he could, but all that came of his efforts was sweat percolating underneath his plaid button-down that he couldn't wipe away. Dread started creeping into his brain, and he had no idea what to expect next.

After a few minutes passed, Ryan heard faint music. A low, sexy pulse of some electronica music, coming from the hallway where his feet were on display. He looked up at the gallery camera, and suddenly saw a large group of men enter, most wearing formal clothes, all of them wearing masks like they were at a masquerade. A waiter in a white tuxedo (and no shoes, Ryan noticed), walked around with champagne, and the gentlemen milled about the large gallery space, joking and talking amongst themselves. Ryan tried screaming for help, hoping that his words could somehow escape through his pantlegs and out to the room at large, but this proved futile -- he couldn't be heard over the throbbing dance music playing for these well-to-dos. Ryan eyed the monitor closely, and couldn't make a single woman at all -- just all guys. Ryan was trying desperately to wrap his head around what was going on.

Suddenly, a hand had placed itself around his foot, grabbing at the sole of his shoe, the hand forcibly moving his foot back and forth for no discernible reason, perhaps to examine it.

"Hey pervert! Let the fuck go!" Ryan shouted, but nothing came of it. He tried to determine who was holding onto his foot, but those masks were making it close to impossible for Ryan to determine who was manhandling his left clodhopper. Suddenly another hand began tracing the rim of Ryan's right shoe sole, going around and around at a deliberately slow pace, as if savoring, perhaps guessing was underneath. That hand then began tapping the sole with his fingers, playfully, as if trying to tickle Ryan's foot through his shoe. Ryan fidgeted as much as he could, trying to retract his foot through the wall hole, but to no avail. Looking at the monitor, it seemed that the people standing around his feet in the gallery were quite enjoying the boy's reactions. Before more people could gather, some sort of whistle went off and all the masked men met down at one end of the gallery, as the mingling time was over -- they were now going to be traveling in a group. Ryan didn't like the look of this at all.

He saw the men gather around one pair of feet sticking out from the gallery, and they were gathered so tight that Ryan couldn't make out exactly what was happening on the monitors. Minutes were passing and all he could see was the occasional reaction from the group -- usually something that pleased them. They stuck by that pair of feet for about 20 minutes or so, and each minute they were there Ryan's brain raced around with numerous nightmare scenarios, many way more gruesome, graphic, and bloody than they should be. Suddenly, the men moved on to the next pair of feet in the gallery. Just barely, Ryan could see that the pair of feet they were previously around were now bare and exposed -- a pair of sneakers were strewn about on the ground, and the socks were nowhere to be found (although maybe the guy went sockless? They were skater shoes, so that would make some sense ...). The guys seemed to be equally taken with their new set of feet sticking out of the wall, and judging from the monitors, there was one other guy between where Ryan was now and where the group was. He watched the men closely, trying to see if could figure out anything that they were doing. Suddenly one shoe came flying up from the huddled group of masked men, landing behind them -- apparently, they were feeling a bit whimsical now ... or maybe just somewhat drunk. Ryan wasn't sure if this scared him or not.

The group moved from to the next set after about 10 minutes of playing with the last pair, and Ryan's whole back tensed up -- they were one away from him. Ryan still couldn't make out exactly what was happening, but given how much closer they were to him, Ryan could make out occasional glimpses of that poor soul's soles on the monitor. Depending on where the masked men moved, he could see the feet being touched and handled ... and the toes distorting in a spectacular fashion, as if they were trying to get away from something or ... oh dear god ...

... tickled.

Ryan had never been so scared. He struggled violently once more, but, once again, was greeted with nothing more than his body releasing more hot, sticky sweat. Ryan was the kind of guy who rarely took off his socks, much less his shoes -- a scroll through his pictures on Facebook never once shows his feet bare or exposed in any way (the few times he wore sandals, he made sure no camera was anywhere in sight). As such, his soles were very soft, pale pink, and, very, very tender. Tickling positively drove him mental, and he's attacked those who've tickled him before. Right here, right now, however, he didn't have that kind of defense. In fact, right now, he was completely helpless.

The men seemed to be finished with the latest pair of tender goslings, and soon formed a circle around Ryan's feet, which were twitching with nervous anticipation. Ryan's back somehow tensed up even more, tighter than a thousand wound coils. He eyed the monitor very closely, and at first, the masked men were just ... standing around his feet. They seemed to just be watching his shoe-covered feet nervously twitch and move like frightened animals in a corner. Every time Ryan got self-conscious about it, his nervousness just made it worse, his sneakered feet fidgeting -- perhaps even groveling -- before the mysterious men. Then, with no warning, a hand began caressing the instep of his shoe. Ryan tried to hit it away with his other foot, but it's at that moment that someone else's hand grabbed his other foot, rendering it immobile.

The fondling of his left sneakered instep continued on for some time -- whoever was doing this was quite enjoying it. Then, the man's index finger went underneath the tongue of his shoe, his other hand grabbed the heel, and in one quick motion, that shoe came right off. Ryan couldn't see what happened on the monitor, as the men's faces were now out of frame, but it was obvious that someone was sniffing the collected foot sweat inside his shoe. Before Ryan even knew what was happening, the other shoe came off, and now Ryan's sweaty feet were down to those dark gray socks. The moisture from his socks suddenly became apparent once the cool air of the room hit his helpless dogs, and, strangely, that made Ryan feel even more vulnerable.

His toes curled, as if in fear, and there was some minor deal of movement around the men. One hand descended onto his right foot, cradling it, while another set of hands grabbed his left foot and began kneading his soles, attempting to massage it. His right socked sole was now just being fondled, stroked, caressed, while the kneading continued on his left. Ryan couldn't do much of anything, and found the sensation ... weird. These guys were ... trying to please his feet? Against his will? Ryan's neurons were firing but all that came out were dull sparks: he couldn't figure out what the fuck was going on.

Suddenly, the man who was caressing his foot got down to his knees, so he was eye-level with Ryan's socked toes. Ryan couldn't make out much, but all he could tell was that the man was younger, handsome even. The man, still wearing his mask, pressed his nose right into the base of Ryan's big toe and inhaled. Ryan could feel the air rushing in between his big and first toe, and it was odd, to say the least. From what he could gather from the video feed, the young man really seemed to enjoy it, and proceeded to do it again. Another man bent down next to Ryan's other socked foot and after lightly caressing the sensitive sides of his left clodhopper, leaned up a bit and proceeded to suck on Ryan's big toe through the sock. Ryan's foot immediately tried to fidget away, but the guy's hands firmly held the foot in place. The sucking was slow, deliberate, and very, very sensual. Suddenly, his moist left sock was starting to get damp, and he had no idea what to think. Ryan may have even felt a tingle inside himself -- one of *those* tingles -- but immediately ignored it.

As the intensity of the toe sucking increased, fingers reached out to the rim of his left gray sock and began slowly snaking it off the boy's foot. Ryan desperately fought this as much as he could but it was pointless: the sock was off in seconds. His toes instinctively flexed a bit, adjusting to their new freedom, and just like that, his much-sniffed right sock also came off. His bare feet were sticking out the other end of a wall, and whatever the men on the other side were seeing, it was quite obvious that they liked it.

Being barefoot, his left toes especially moist from the soaked-through saliva of his mysterious foot friend, Ryan had never felt so naked in his life. This includes the times he was actually naked in the locker rooms at high school, yet for some reason to have his shoes and socks forcibly removed at the whim of what seemed like a dozen professional foot fetishizers ... it was almost too much for him. While he wished he could've retracted his feet into the wall before, he now simply wished he could pass out and have the whole thing over with.

That, however, was not the case. The two men who were already kneeling in front of his feet were then joined by two other men who knelt down. They seemed to be evenly-divided: two men to a foot. Ryan's toes once again curled in terror, and even Ryan's own face grimaced a bit in anticipation. Then, after each silent second creeped by as if it was an hour in length, the licking began.

Tongues planted themselves at various parts of his feet and proceeded to slither up his soles, across his too-sensitive tops, around his heel, and oh, especially at the toes. Whoever was working the toes of each foot were clearly enjoying themselves, their moist, horny tongues savoring each and every flavor, texture, and detail. Those tongues polished the toenails, lapped at the toepads, and slithered in-between each toe like a hungry snake. The tongues sneaking between each toe began driving Ryan bonkers: they were so wet they seemed to just glide, tickling him intensely. Ryan didn't want to be tickled, and fought it as much as he could, his face distorting and his arms moving at sharp angles, despite being tightly bound. Ryan closed his eyes and clenched his lip as the warm tongues played with his index toe, his too-helpless pinkie toe, and the base of his big toe, but as their speed increased, so did the moist tickles, the little taste bumps on each tongue scraping at the sensitive spaces in-between each digit.

The worshiper on his left foot then did something utterly devious: his tongue darted in and out of the spaces between Ryan's middle toes over and over again, quickly, quickly, tickling more and more each time. Suddenly, Ryan couldn't fight it anymore: the laughter burst out of him, and he resembled a Muppet gone wild. His body seizured to each side, he leaned forward as quickly as he could before slamming back down again, his body doing everything it could to combat the laughter issuing forth from his mouth, but it was all a wasted effort. The other tongues circled his heels and slowly traced his arches, but tongues between his toes were tickling way too much, saliva dripping down the sides of his feet like a melted ice cream cone. Ryan's eyes were firmly shut, as if holding back tears. His head titled back, and his high-pitched cackles came jutting out. Mixed in with them were please of "Stop!" "Don't!" and the ever-classic "It tickles!!" Of course, with a wall between him and his tormentors, Ryan's pleas fell on deaf ears. If those mysterious men even could hear the boy, they'd probably just be turned on by what they heard: honest-to-goodness helpless laughter. Not a firm enjoyable chuckle, or high-pitched whine, no; genuine laughter. Laughter that had to be forcibly removed from its subject, which sounded like it'd do anything for its torment to stop. It was laughter that couldn't enjoy itself; it was laughter that was forced into being laughter.

A half-hour passed.

The slurping stopped, as if all at once. Ryan's feet were simply coated in saliva, his toes exhausted from their wiggling. Ryan's own chest began heaving heavily, his voice scratchy and hoarse, his body spewing out the occasional laughter aftershock completely against his will. With sweat forming on his brow that he positively couldn't wipe away even if he wanted to, all Ryan wanted to do was pass out. He was so weak, he couldn't even fight back when he felt the guys doing something to his toes, as if wrapping something around each one. He knew it was pointless to fight at this time -- it's like his own feet were no longer his.

Then, the cinch came. His feet were now completely flexed back. Ryan looked at the monitor: on the wall in the gallery, there were eight hooks located right above where Ryan's feet were sticking out of the wall. Every toe was tied back to a hook, all seemingly using the same piece of rope, which explains why when they cinched it tight, all his toes moved back at once. The cruel masked men, however, left his pinkie toe on each side completely free to move, giving him the horrible illusion of movement. Ryan, fearful, watched the monitor ahead, doing his best to curl his toes even a half-inch -- and they couldn't even do that. He was completely immobile, save his pinkie toes, which flexed and moved just a little bit, all cute and helpless. He then saw that two of the masked men had grabbed feathers and were nearing closer and closer to his immobile feet. Ryan screamed once more, and then ... he felt it.

The tiny scrape of the tip of a feather against the ball of his left foot. It ... almost didn't tickle. It was so slight, indiscernible. He felt a light wisp on his left foot, but, again, it was fleeting. Slowly but surely, the feather strokes became more apparent, just calmly tracing the balls of his feet on a horizontal line. Wisp. Wisp. Wiiiiiiiiiiisp. It was excruciating. In fact, this was worse than tickling: it was "almost tickling", and it was putting Ryan's exhausted mind in a state of perpetual tension, preparing itself for the full-blown tickles that weren't coming. This went on for five excruciating minutes, and Ryan's feet began to tingle with anticipation. "Just tickle me already!!" he kept thinking, but all he was greeted with was Wisp. Wiiiisp. Wisp. Another three minutes passed, and Ryan was about to lose it.

Then, the feathers stopped. Out of nowhere, a single fingernail glided up the arches of his left foot, and Ryan jolted. It was so unexpected, so -- AHHHH! It happened on his right foot. Then another on his right foot. And then Ryan realized his fears had come true: the tickling had begun.

A bevy of fingers descended on his bound soles, and they were enjoying their soft and fleshy playthings. Some fingers scraped, some lightly poked, some traced circles, some scratched the sides of his feet, some wiggled in front of his toes, and all of them fucking tickled. His bare size 11s were on fire with electricity, processing through a million different ticklish sensations at once. His nerve endings were practically screaming at him, but all he could do was just unleash more torrents of laughter. Tickly tickles. Ticklish tickles. Tickle tickle tickles -- this was all his brain seemed to be capable of thinking. The more he laughed, the worse he got. Every time his lungs drew in to catch his breath, a finger went horizontal across his toepads and a laugh jumped into his lungs. Ryan's brain was buckling under the pressure. The person on his right foot apparently was trying to spell out letters on his soles, his fingernail no doubt leaving a trail of white as it drew across his pink soles, spelling out Q's and fancy S's with too many loops. Ryan pretty much went on cackle auto-pilot. His sanity slowly began to slip, and had he known this was going to continue on for 20 minutes more, his brain would've prepared itself more.

In Ryan's feathery fever dream, years must've passed. His brain had lost all sense of space and time -- he could be a medieval knight for all he knew. The only thoughts that were going through his brain consisted of only one or two syllables: Tickle. Feet. Toes. Tickle. Laugh. Lungs. Water. Ticklisssssssh. Tickley! Tickles. Tooooooooes. Feet. Scratchy. Laughy. In truth, the tickling had actually stopped for a few minutes, but Ryan's brain didn't even detect it until long after.

When his eyes readjusted to the monitors above him, he could see that the men had moved on to maybe three other pairs of feet since he last checked. Ryan couldn't make sense of many things right now, but all he could tell was that the other poor souls (and soles) locked in the gallery right now did not have to suffer as long as his did. While all the men were huddled around their latest foot toy, one of the masked men broke from the pack and seemed to approach Ryan's feet. A hand reached down and briefly tickled Ryan's left heel. Instinctively, it flinched. A feather then came out and proceeded to tickle only that left pinkie toe -- it tried its damndest to escape but that toe was too limited in its movements to do anything. It just danced with the feather, accepted its tickles, and only pretended to escape. For some reason, having his pinkie toes free to move about despite their limited capacity to do so was probably the most frustrating part of the whole thing. The masked man knelt down next to his bound feet, and, from what Ryan could tell through his fuzzy eyesight (hard to regain vision after you've teared up from laughing so much), that man was the same one who so passionately sucked his big toe through his sock earlier. The man leaned in, sniffed that left foot, and then planted a simple kiss on Ryan's left sole, then the right. The masked man reached into his pocket and pulled out what appeared to be a black sharpie marker, and proceeded to press it into Ryan's right sole, and really began to write something. The letters tickled, and Ryan's last reserve of laughter just jumped out of him. This was weak laughter now: high-pitched and craggily. Laughter of the truly defeated. The slightly moist marker swooped in and out, made all sorts of shapes, and simply made Ryan go bonkers just one more time. FUCK Ryan hated whoever was doing this to him right now. When the marker seemed to reach the bottom of his left foot, the ticklish writing stopped. The young masked man got up and walked back to where the rest of the group was torturing some other helpless young man. Ryan, about to pass out, still managed to look up at his bound boyfeet on the monitor and make out what was written:

"I hope you learned your lesson, Ryan. Don't make us come back for you ... unless you want to join us ..." There was a smiley face at the end of that sentence, as well as the image of a crudely-drawn feather across the bottom of Ryan's heel. Ryan tried to make sense of it, but his brain couldn't fight his physical exhaustion much longer. At long last, Ryan -- with his feet in another room and his toes tied back, moist marker ink still drying on his soles -- passed out.

+ + +

Ryan's eyelids fought very hard to remain closed, but Ryan could sense himself gradually waking up. All his body was telling him right now was how much it hurt, especially his feet. Ryan looked around: he was still wearing the same plaid shirt as before and the same pants, but he was very much barefoot. He looked around: he was in his own room again, but not underneath the covers, actually on top of them. Suddenly, Ryan shot up: he instantly remembered everything that happened to him immediately before: his feet in a wall, his socked toes being sucked on, a feather teasing his pinkie toes with absolute relish, him completely losing his mind. Ryan instinctively grabbed the soles of his feet with his hands, as if to protect them. Then he calmed down a bit -- was that all a dream? Did ... did that all really happen? After all, his toes still hurt a lot ...

Ryan looked around his room, just to make sure everything was OK, and then noticed that his computer monitor had a note taped to it. He got off of the bed, his bare feet making contact with his too-familiar carpet at long last, comforting him, and he leaned forward, eying what was taped there. It seemed to be a card of some sort, and all it said on the front was "You are invited ..."

The boy then opened up the card, and couldn't believe what he saw inside ...

THE DREAMS PT 1 & 2

+ + +

What do you do with the most unlikely of fetish finds? The lead character of this story actually circled around the vague periphery of "The Roommate" from My, What Ticklish Feet You Have, *and participated in the occasional tickle (never anything serious, just playful). In truth, the person whom this character is based off of is one of the more sexually conservative people that I know, and even though he's straight as an arrow, I could tell there's just the slightest hint of heteroflexibility in his sexual history. Terrible person I am, I always, always wanted to play with that slight bit of willingness inside of him (largely due to the fact that yes, as shy and reluctant as he'd be, I'd totally be able to get him to enjoy it), but the true reality is that he's closed himself off too much to such explorations. With some as determined and direct as he is, I figured it might be interesting to plug him in to a manipulative story concept I had been kicking around for a while, one where erotic dreams are forced into his head, slightly altering his outlook on just about everything. The resulting tale was so epic it was initially published in two parts, and here they are, together at last, for your delightful enjoyment ...*

PART ONE

The blade slashed furiously.

Grunts and sweats followed, dead vines littering his path. Michael slashed again and again, each swish of the blade reflecting off coins of sunlight for split seconds. Michael wiped his sweaty brow, his deep breaths mixing in with the hot jungle air. He had never felt more exhausted in his life, but knew he had to keep on moving. He had come half way across the world for this hunt, and he wasn't going to stop now.

Michael wasn't one for detours, excuses, or giving up easily. It was mixed into his Swedish heritage (and at age 26, it was more prominent than ever, he felt), which explained his no-bullshit approach to just about everything. He stood there shining like the reedy hero he was: circular explorer hat on, leather backpack strapped across his tan-shirted back, thick brown hiking shorts firmly fitted and his size 11s fit nicely in a pair of gray wool socks and industrial-strength dark brown hiking boots -- nothing was going to stop him. His exposed appendages were coated with sunscreen, as his pale-white skin burned quite easily when left unattended. With each wipe of his brow, however, he felt that he was losing sense of what, exactly what he was after. All he knew about now was one thing and one thing only: the hunt. That's what he lived for, and right now, he was completely in his element.

Another slash from his machete sent shards of green everywhere; vines became confetti. After walking through the thick of the jungle for what seemed like hours, Michael finally came to an open clearing, grass barely rising up to his knees as his eyes caught a glimpse of the setting sun, making the tops of the trees glow a distinct orange. It was a glorious sight to see, and standing there, drinking it all in, Michael felt at rest, at peace. This was a moment he didn't even know he was craving, but relished it none-the-less. He let out a pleasant sigh. Everything, right now, felt right.

Then, out of the corner of his eye, he saw something. His eyes darted, his body tensed. He was afraid he had been spotted by some sort of animal. He turned around sharply -- nothing in his sight. He turned back towards the clearing, and jumped: it was staring at him. His grip on the machete slipped ever so slightly upon seeing it. It was ... a vine. A large, green vine that was pointed directly at him. The end of it wasn't a thin tip, though: it was rounded, like the end of a thick sausage, the whole vine itself having the thickness of a human arm. It was a big, big vine -- and it was ... well, looking at him. It was like a snake had descended from the trees, but no, it was very clearly a vine. It wavered in the air, slithering, almost, cautiously eying the human in front of it. Michael ... didn't know what to think. Although he was initially quite scared, he sensed that this very much was something that was ... living. He took a step to the left, and the vine followed him. He took a step to the right, and it followed him again. Michael's face scrunched -- he wasn't sure what to do.

Moments passed as the two life forms stared at each other. Neither was moving -- just staring at the mystery that was the other. Michael then did a very diplomatic move -- he slowly put his machete down on the jungle floor. He stood up again. The vine "looked" at the machete on the ground and then placed its gaze right back on Michael. Once again, Michael went the diplomatic route and slowly extended his hand towards the vine-thing. At first, looking at the fingertips, the vine recoiled a bit, and then, cautiously, seemed to almost "sniff" his hand. It very lightly brushed against it -- and nothing happened. The vine (which Michael still couldn't figure out where exactly it was coming from) then rubbed up against his hand, and did so again. It was almost like a cat looking for chin scratches -- the vine was enjoying this contact. It slowly got closer to Michael's body, and was now genuinely, almost playfully interested in him. It swirled around his face, eyed his clothing, his boots, his hat -- everything. "Um ... OK" was pretty much the only thought that was going through Michael's mind at the moment. If this was first contact with some otherworldly thing, well, it certainly could've gone worse.

Even as the vine began eying him, the "face" of the vine, as indistinct as it was, began playfully poking him at times, seeing what was in a front pocket of his shirt, nudging his backpack -- it was getting a feel for whatever this two-legged thing was. What was odd, however, was when it looked at Michael's shorts. It seemed to take a rather strong interest in them, waving around left to right to get a view at them from all sides. It then playfully poked Michael in the crotch a bit. Michael, being Michael, stepped back. "OK ... that's ... a bit too far," he said out loud. Yet the vine was undeterred: it poked him again, this time on the inner thigh. It didn't hurt at all (it was a vine after all), but it did kind of tickle a bit. Michael again stepped back and said "OK, no. That's a no-no place." The vine, however, didn't seem to care.

In a lightning fast move, the vine suddenly went up Michael's left pant leg and underneath his boxers. It was so quick Michael barely had time to react, much less let out the yelp that he did. The soft face of the vine was suddenly touching his balls, and jumping away as best as he could, Michael fell to the ground, but didn't shake the vine. He felt something moist underneath his boxers all of a sudden, and panicked: the thing was going to eat him! Sadly, that wasn't true, however, but the "mouth" of the vine opened up, and immediately swallowed Michael's balls and cock in one foul swoop. What was weird, however, was that whatever liquids were inside the mouth of this thing, the second they touched his balls and cock, he became instantaneously horny. His arms were holding onto the vine entering his pantleg, desperately trying to get it out, but right now, his cock was filled with what felt like a year's worth of pent-up horny tingles (which was weird -- he jerked off just two nights ago without a problem). This moist mouth suddenly did a "suck" on his member, and holy shit, Michael had never felt anything like it. It was like liquid electricity. His cock, his balls, his entire sexual being shot to life, awakened like a thunderbolt. Another suck occurred, and Michael's dick was already beet-red. While his brain did everything it could to still fight off this intruder, he was receiving signals unlike anything he had ever encountered before, signals that coded the words "tingle", "fuck", "tickle", and "cum". This was all happening so quickly. Too quickly. There is no kind of panic like a horny panic.

The ripping sound was insanely loud: the leg of Michael's shorts was ripping, the large vine seemingly wanting to rip the things off just by flexing. Even with both hands around the green sexual menace attacking him, he couldn't get the vine out. Another suck occurred, and Michael practically moaned. Suddenly there was a playful bump in his ribs. Michael laughed a bit, then panicked: there was another vine staring at him! He did a quick double take, but suddenly there was another ticklish bump on the other side of his ribs. Michael looked and saw yet another vine. Two other vines were now eying their prey. Michael was about to scream or punch or do something, but before he could: SUUUUUUCK. A deep throb was felt again on his steel-hard cock, and Michael almost had to close his eyes -- it was that intense. Even with the main vine wrapped around his cock and balls, some of that horny liquid it was emanating began dripping down underneath Michael's balls, slowly into his gooch, and everything that liquid touched made those areas get all the hornier. Michael didn't have much time to enjoy it though: the other two vines began poking his chest and ribs again, really tickling him. Michael fucking *hated* being tickled, but the two other vines seemed to really be loving it. Even as he vainly tried to fight the ticklevines off, he felt yet another vine ease its way into his left sock, pulling both the sock and tightly-tied boot off his left foot. Michael let out a "No!" in-between chortled laughs, but before he could finish, another vine was working his right foot. Two more vines wrapped around his wrists and pulled the boy taught. The tickling of his ribs continued, one of the vines going in through his shirt sleeve to try and play with his pits and hard nipples. The shoes were now off, and Michael was barefoot on the floor of the jungle, his pale white feet flailing for just a few moments before those vines near his feet just swallowed his feet whole. Much like the vine around cock, his feet were plunged into a moist, sensual place, that horny goo now sliding in-between his toes, tickling him and teasing him and sending him into ecstasy. Another suck came on the one on his cock, and Michael couldn't take it anymore. He arched his back, lost complete control of his body, precum oozing out his red cockhead, his curved cock trembling, trembling, trembling ...

+ + +

"Ahhhhhhhhhhhhhhh!!" Michael screamed, sitting straight up to attention, panting. Cool air blew across his sweaty face. Michael looked around: he was in his bedroom in his apartment. It was the dead of night. He took a few panicked breaths, and then slowly realized what had just happened: he awoke from a dream. A very, very strange dream. He heard the dull hum of his air conditioner permeate the air. Michael's shoulders loosened just a bit: it was all a dream. That's all it was. His pants turned into simple sighs -- but something didn't feel right. His eyebrow arched. He lifted up his bed sheets, and saw ... what looked like a weeks worth of cum staining them. Holy shit, he must've shot rockets of cum, as his sheets were drenched, his crotch caked with dry sperm. Did ... did he just cum from having a dream where vines were sucking his dick, toes, and nipples? What the fuck kind of dream was this? Michael couldn't even begin to figure out what just happened. He slowly got out of bed, almost as if on autopilot, his bare feet touching the chilled hard-paneled floor of his apartment. He walked to the bathroom, cleaned himself off, and went back into bed (sleeping over his cum-stained sheet for the time being). His mind was still racing around, doing its best to figure out what the hell just happened, but more importantly, his eyes were droopy and heavy. Confused and perplexed, his mind slowly shut down and Michael drifted off to sleep once again.

The next morning, Michael went about his daily routine at a somewhat slower pace, his mind trying to decipher what last night meant. It all felt very surreal, very strange, and very much not in his usual "routine" at all. Why the fuck would he have a dream about a giant pair of vines getting him off? As he stood there by the kitchen counter waiting for his coffee to finish, T-shirt and red pajama pants on, his raw toes doing all that they could to ignore the cold that was seeping up from the morning floor, his mind kept drifting back to those too-vivid images that plagued his mind from last night. Often with dreams, he would try to piece things together, remember elements or themes but never fully grasping a full narrative of what transpired. Here, however, he remembered every detail clear as day. For some reason, he kept going back to that feeling of the vines swallowing his feet, that moisture running down between his toes, tingling and exciting his skin whilst tickling the whole way through.

Michael snapped his head back to attention -- he wasn't going to keep daydreaming like he was, especially about that. His coffee finished, but as he went to grab a mug, he stopped moving, shocked at what he saw: he was tenting in his pajama pants. He was unbelievably rock hard and didn't even realize it. Was it from thinking of the dream too much? Michael shook it off. Today was a day for no distractions. Especially one as "private" as that.

Some 12 hours later, Michael came back to his apartment. Wearing nothing but a T-shirt, tan cargo shorts, and sneakers without socks, he was beat, having just done a nine-hour light hang for a local school's assembly tomorrow, along with programming and cue-to-cuing everything that needed to be done before Friday. He broke out a Hot Pocket, grabbed himself a beer, and sat down in front of his computer, loading up *World of Warcraft* for the umpteenth time, using it to cool down after a long an grueling day. Some e-mails were sent, more drinks were had, and before long, Michael was in bed, dozing away before tomorrow's workload weighed down on him.

What Michael didn't know, however, was what devious thing I had in store for him tonight.

+ + +

The air smelled of hot jazz. The nighttime city skyline didn't look real: it was all dark blue paint strokes, Van Gogh auras and artistic splashes. It was like walking through a painting, except the whole world was a painting. People moved along -- the people looked like real flesh-and-blood people -- but everything else took on a post-bop hue, looking like pastels but smelling like the best parts of a 2AM jazz club. Michael wasn't as much walking as floating. He felt the air move around him, and began to notice his dress: he was completely bare-chested, wearing dark blue jeans, and dark brown leather flip-flops as well. This is a look that Michael would probably never have pulled off in real life, but here, in this world, it made perfect sense. He floated along into a nearby bar, filled with pool tables and overhanging lights. He went up to the bar and raised his hand, not saying a word -- a beer was instantly handed to him. He sat there at the barstool, chest naked to the world, and no one seemed to mind. There seemed to be only one or two people in the club anyways, but they seemed to be always in shadows, paying no mind to anyone but themselves. So there was Michael drinking at the bar, flip-flops dangling off his feet as he sat on a barstool. Despite his lack of a shirt, he felt weirdly ... comfortable. It was a surrealistic sight to behold.

The bar's front door swung open. Michael's head swung around and saw that it was ... me. His friend from all the way back in college. I walked in fully clothed, my 6' stature almost matching his. I had on no jacket or cap like some of the other bar inhabitants had, just myself looking casual. Michael instantly recognized me as I walked up to the bar, gesturing to the bartender to get me a drink as well.

"Hey there Mikey Mike."

"Hey," he responded, surprised to see me there.

"How goes things?"

"Um, well ... I seem to be missing a shirt."

"I've noticed," I quipped.

"Um," he paused, gathering his bearings, "where are we?"

"Only the coolest part of town," I started, "where dreams come true and lives are changed."

"... are you working for this bar?" asked Michael, dead serious.

"Heh, no I'm not, Michael. But you know what sounds good right about now?"

"What?" he inquired.

"A game of pool," I said.

"Um ... OK." He got up with me, as if on friendship autopilot, both carrying beers in our hand, as we got to the pool table underneath a single hanging bulb, and it looked paint stroke blue just like everything else in this place. Michael started looking for a pool cue, but I stopped him: "No need for that, Michael. All you'll need are these ..." I held up a pair of jet-black bracelets for him.

"Um ... what are these?"

"Try 'em on!"

Without hesitating, Michael put the bracelets on and ... well, they were snug.

"How they fit?" I asked, smiling.

"Um, good," he started. "I just ... don't know what they're for."

I laughed a bit. "Heh ... let me show ya. Lie down on the table for me."

Being dream logic, any pretense about a pool game was immediately forgotten. Michael hopped up on the table and laid himself down, his ankles overhanging on one end while his eyes stared up at the bare lightbulb directly above him (it didn't blind him however -- it seemed to be quite diffused). I leaned over his bare-chested, sandal-clad body and simply said "Move."

Michael tried -- yet he couldn't. He tried lifting up his arms, but those bracelets suddenly felt like they weighed hundreds of pounds. Michael tried lifting his legs up, but suddenly its like his jeans were attached to the table -- all he could do was simply wiggles his toes, causing his flip-flops to slap against his bare heels a bit. If this were real life, he'd be furious right now, but being a dream, he seemed to feel indifferent to the whole thing. I reached over and placed both of his nipples between my thumb and index finger, and began lightly rubbing, flicking his niptips ever so softly just to see what kind of response I could get out of him. Although his body tensed at first, it soon recognized that all my fingers were trying to do was pleasure him, and suddenly each nip-flick felt like an erotic little spark, like a flint misfire on a cigarette lighter, teasing him oh so wonderfully. Flick, flick, flick they went. Michael, still confused on what exactly was happening, started giving in to the feeling a bit, his nipples starting to harden up and protrude out of his chest as the flicking continued, each erotic little spark adding to the stirrings that were going on in his crotch. It felt like a dull firework went off in the base of his cock, his hardon slowly coming into fruition. It was perhaps even more sensational for him due to the fact that only his nipples were being touched -- not even his chest or stomach or pits were getting the slightest sensation of feeling. Those dull fireworks felt more and more colorful with each burst, his cock already at standing attention, pulsing underneath that blue denim fabric. Whatever was happening, Michael was assuredly enjoying it.

I stopped playing with my mantoy and proceeded to walk down the end of the pool table where his sandaled feet dangled over the edge, cute and helpless. I began tapping and flicking the sandals, occasionally poking his bared soles while I talked:

"You got some nice feet there, Michael."

"And you have a male foot fetish if I'm not mistaken, yes?", he inquired, no anger anywhere in his voice.

"Yes I do, Michael," I started. "You remember college so well."

"Well, it's kind of a hard thing to forget."

"Oh I know, but, allow me to toss a theory out there: you have never been one to think of feet as being sexy, correct?"

I fondled his flips a bit more. "Um, yes, that would be correct," he replied.

"Well that I understand. From the outside, having a foot fetish must seem like the strangest, damndest thing. Someone getting turned on by the mere sight of someone else's exposed toes? Doesn't make sense. Then again, if people like you get turned on by a nice show of cleavage, an exposed pair of breasts, a nice pair of legs -- it's really not all that different deep down, just not as commonly accepted. However, what people don't know is that much like those other coveted areas, feet can be pleasured in ways that are highly, highly erotic."

"Oh?" the immobile boy asked.

"Oh yes," I continued, slowly removing his flimsy flip-flops from his pale, hairless feet. "Yes. Mind if I demonstrate?"

"Well ... I'm not going anywhere," he said.

I grinned. Two soft slaps were heard as the sandals landed on the floor. I knelt down, and immediately inserted my tongue in-between his toes, slathering in-between them, licking their undersides, sucking on them, occasionally licking his sensitive arches just for the hell of it. Immobile Michael flinched, twitched, and let out light gasps -- this was a completely new experience for him. Sometimes my tongue waggled about the base of his toes just so that tickles radiated through him, adding to those tingles he was undoubtedly feeling. Sometimes I would do a slow lick of his heel, dragging that tongue across those arches and up to the those toes so that every groove and taste bump on my tongue could be felt by his too-soft skin, tickling and pleasuring him in equal measure. My tongue lapped up the tops of his feet, gliding all over, and then I went back to lightly sucking on each toe, going out of my way to make sure each and every one was properly serviced, no inch of his feet left without moisture by the time I was done.

The best part of the whole thing, though, was his reactions. The toes involuntarily flexing, the occasional quick-pant, the random groan of pleasure that would emerge -- it was all new, terrifyingly sexy territory for Michael. And then he felt it -- the first fingernail scratch across his left heel. He flinched a bit, I laughed a little, and then the attack began: ten fingernails sliding, grooving, flicking, poking and tickling his heels. Michael laughed in surprise, his toes flexed, curled, and drew circles in the air as they tried to escape their torment, but it was no use: the rapid, teasing scratches continued. Slowly, the fingernails tickling his heels went up his feet, across the tender arches, to the balls of his feet, the base of his toes, the tips of his toes -- a thousand ticklish slashes all hitting him at once. Michael's ribcage jolted, popped, and tried to escape, but the tickles kept coming. His bare fleshy soles were a delivery system for devious, teasing tickles, and the rest of his body could only contort and twist to try and escape it, even if the results amounted to nothing more than constant, unwilling laughs launching out of from his mouth. I loved taking my index finger and poking in-between each pair of toes, swirling it around before moving on to the next toeslot. I was fucking loving this.

"Your toes are sexy when they wiggle, Michael," I said in a teasing voice. All that Michael responded with was more unbridled laughter. I next cradled his heels in my hand, fingers along the sides as my thumbs scratched his heels and the base of his arches -- oh man did he hate this! His toes scrunched in a much as they could as if they somehow could bend down far enough to stop my fingers -- but they couldn't. It was really cute seeing how hard his body was trying to avoid the tickles, flashes of ticklish lightning setting his feet ablaze with tingles and tickles. I continued scratching his soles with my thumbnails for about 20 minutes -- there wasn't a moment when he wasn't laughing hysterically during it.

I stopped, and Michael panted, those occasional aftershocks of laughter coming out in bits and waves. I walked over to where Michael could clearly see me.

"So ... ticklish much?"

"Fuck you," me panted out.

My fingers traced across his chest and down to his belt buckle, then slowly, forcefully traced his zipperline, feeling his still-hard manhood inside. "I think you like it when I tickle your feet,

Michael." I scratched his shaft through the jeans, and his whole body tensed again, those half-moans coming out of his mouth seemingly against his will. I then stopped and looked at his bare chest, soaked in sweat. I grinned again.

"Michael, answer me this question honestly: do you *like* it when I play with your feet?"

"Um ..." he panted, "I um ... I don't ..."

I started scratching his shaft and cockhead through the jeans.

"Michael, do you *like it* when I play with your feet?"

"Um ... I mean ... god keep doing that ... I ... kind of ... I ..."

"Michael, do you want me to really, really play with your big bare feet one more time?

The scratching was causing his shaft to pump and twitch inside its denim prison.

"I ... yes."

"What part do you like the most, Michael?"

"I ... I liked it when ... fuck yes ... when you were licking my toes ..."

"Good boy, Michael," I said as I stopped the scratching and went down to his feet. "Then you're going to really like this."

With feverish, horny relish, I began tonguing the tips of his toes. Michael shuddered a bit, but his toes didn't clench -- they seemed to almost lean into it. I began licking his entire foot from sole to toes again, lapping it over and over, and slowly, his feet began to grow. Michael barely even noticed however, as his feet slowly growing in size was about equivalent to how horny he was feeling. They were now size 12s, then 14s, then 17s ... they kept on growing with each lick. "Fuck yes," he mumbled, my tongue now resting in-between his big toe and his index toe, slathering back and forth and back and forth in that big sexy toeslot, tickling and teasing and moistening all along. The tickles felt good, the warm, wet tongue felt good, his raging hardon felt great. Slowly his feet got bigger and bigger, his toes plumper, my licking all the hornier and furiouser. "Yes," he moaned, practically dry humping the air above him, "keep playing with my feet. Keep licking my feet. I love it when you play with my big, bare feet." The humping was intensifying. "Keep going," I shouted. He closed his eyes and moaned some more: "I love it when you lick my feet! KEEP PLAYING WITH MY ... "

+ + +

"... FEET!" he shouted as he sprung to attention, bolt upright in his bed. Michael was sweating, panting, and ... awake. He looked around his darkened room and ... saw nothing. His body was heaving and heaving, his chest taking in bucket breaths, but ... it was all a dream as far as he was concerned. He closed his eyes and took a breath ... and then he felt it. His crotch was sticky again. He must've cum even worse than the night previous. He didn't even need to look -- he already knew he was going to have to take this sheets and put them on a double-cycle to get them properly clean. Again, it felt like he had just unloaded a month's worth of seed -- but how could this happen two nights in a row? What was wrong? He went to the bathroom to clean himself up, but did so with a strange, nagging doubt floating over him.

The next morning, he sat at his breakfast table, T-shirt, pajama pants, and barefeet, eating his cereal while staring at the back of his cereal box, but not actually looking at anything. His mind was adrift: that surrealistic pool table dream just as vivid as the vine one. While he was disturbed by the fact that he seemed to launch a boatload of cum while in his sleep, he was more disturbed by the fact that I was in that most recent dream, so prominent and realistic, unlike the rest of it. He stopped chewing for a moment and decided to take a risk: he pulled out his cell phone and decided to text me: "Man, you appeared in a very, very weird dream I had last night."

He chewed a few more bites. His phone vibrated there on the table.
He looked at my response and his eyes went wide with terror:

"I thought you'd like it ;-)"

PART TWO

Michael really, really liked this drum pattern. It always lead right into the chorus, which was explosive and fantastic. This is just the kind of music that Michael needed to make sure he didn't kill anyone with a 10-pound light.

Right now, Michael was doing what he did best: crawling around in some theatre scaffolding, affixing lights according to his elaborate lighting design for this show, and doing so while one of his own playlists blasted from the sound booth, a mix of gloriously overblown film scores, strange techno-hybrids, and a few rock songs with quirky lyrics. Michael was at home.

He still had a few stray thoughts enter through his head though, mainly pertaining to what the hell was going on with his batch of surreal, hyper-sexual dreams that he had, one of which featured me quite prominently. He never got a response from me after I told texted him that I certainly hoped he was enjoying those dreams, but whatever: Michael had some work to do, so by gods he would do it. Never hurts to be distracted from curious oddities like that by just diving into some intensive, precise physical labor.

After hanging and positioning about ten more lights, a strange thought occurred to Michael: what show was he lighting? He looked down on the bare black box stage below him, and didn't recognize anything. This wasn't like any set he had seen, and even though he "knew" what he was doing, he had no idea as what he was doing, or why for He looked around at the fellow crewmembers dressed up in typical run-crew black ... and nothing struck him as being familiar. He could see these bodies move around, but their faces were ... hazy, unmemorable. It's almost as if he was surrounded by anonymous figures, indistinct and barely existing.

As he finished screwing in one last night, he heard the light scraping of metal on concrete. Lying practically flat on the metal grid above the stage, he saw a figure drag a simple chair across the black box floor, the metal legs making a sound that cried out for attention. The figure then placed the chair right there on the stage, facing toward the empty house where the audience would sit. Michael then noticed that the figure was also carrying a black bag of some sort. The figure set it down next to the chair, then sat down on the chair, and looked right up at Michael, who gasped a bit:

The figure was me.

"Hello, Michael," I started.

"Um ... hello there." His words had question marks dangling from them.

"How are you?"

"Um, what are you doing here?" This inquisition was starting early.

"Well," I started, rather casually, "I'm here to see you, Michael."

"Um, well, I'm kind of in the middle of a light hang."

"No you're not," I said rather bluntly. "You're in the middle of a glorious, glorious experience. I've been thinking about this for some time, Michael."

"What the hell are you talking about?" he asked, angered by this confusing line of answers I was spewing.

"Well, Michael," I began, grinning the whole time, "you no doubt know of my particular sexual proclivities. I'm intrigued by certain things, and really good at other things. For whatever reason, I'm intensely curious about you right now, Michael. The things I could do to you, the things I could make you feel and experience. It's all very, very intriguing to me. Now, please don't misconstrue what I'm saying: I have no interest in you romantically, and never will. I'm just up for a bit of fun is all. You like a bit of naughty fun now and then, don't you Michael?"

"Yeah, but not like this," he said, almost pressing himself up from the grid ... before realizing he couldn't. He tried bending his knees inward but they weren't moving. He tried moving his arms, but they weren't moving. He looked to his left and his right and saw that some of those anonymous crewmembers had tied poor Michael to the grid spread-eagle using long lengths of thick black shoelace, rendering the wire-y boy completely immobile and several feet above the ground.

"What the hell is this?!" he yelled.

"The start," I quipped. "The start of something I'm going to really, really, really enjoy. Oh, and you will too. In fact, let me have my friends help you out."

I snapped my fingers.

Instantly, the crew up in the grid began working towards undressing Michael only a bit: one unzipped his cargo shorts and pulled his flaccid cock out so it was pointing directly at the black box floor. Two more peeled off his sneakers, revealing sockless feet that could only point out and squirm only so much whilst bound. Another crew member straddled Michael's backside, his hands going underneath Michael's shirt to run along his backside before reaching around to start playing with his nipples, which also pointed directly down to the floor.

"Have at it boys," I declared, and they were off. The two crew members at this feet began to lightly run their fingernails over Michael's deliciously soft feet, already sweaty from a day's work of light hanging, those nails drawing sexy patterns in his sensitive soles, each zig causing him to suddenly cough out an unexpected laughter, each zag making bubbles shoot out his throat entirely against his will. Michael *hated* being tickled, but he kind of had to take it, even as another crew member started flicking his nipples, rubbing their tips, swirling his own fingernail around those nickels of flesh, teasing and toying with the boy with absolute relish. The one who unzipped Michael's pants was taking his time, slowly working his hands across Michael's cheeks, sliding a finger across his gooch, focusing only on teasing the boy, definitely not pleasuring him.

The sudden nature of all of this is what was throwing Michael off. He fought as hard as he could against his nip teasing but goddamn it felt good. His toes scrunched and flailed as much as they can, but each scratch on his bared footflesh felt like lightning being etched into his skin. He came upon the cusp several times: that edge of simply fighting the sensations being force-fed into his system and giving in to the whims of his tormentors. His nips were flicked, his feet were tickled, and -- 'lo and behold -- he was getting a hardon. His brain could barely process all the teases and torments, his ribcage hemorrhaging laughter, everything becoming a weirdly erotic blur all at once.

I snapped my fingers again. Everyone stopped except the guy playing with Michael's nipples.

"I see you're enjoying this, Michael," I noted aloud.

"I ... just ... just ..." Nothing was fully formed in his mind right now. All I know is that the pale-skinned boy was tied in the grid above me and sporting a nice bit of hardon right now.

"Well, Michael, you're undoubtedly aware of my fetishes. Male feet. Tickling. Oh, and this one which is just a fun -- do you happen to know what edging is, Michael?"

"It's ... I dunno it's ..." His words were padded out with canyons of confused silence.

"Well, here, instead of explaining it to you, let me show you."

At this point I reached down to the bag I had placed right next to the chair on the stage floor. I opened it up and pulled out what he thought was a very dirty rag made of material that seemed fancier than a mere rag -- he couldn't make it out (especially with his nips being rubbed every few seconds -- what a terrible distraction!). I also got out a transparent plastic bottle that seemed to contain some sort of golden liquid. I put a good amount of the goop into the center of the rag and held it calmly in my hand.

"You're going to hate this, my friend."

I snapped my fingers.

Suddenly, Michael felt a very, very strange feeling in his cock. It trembled a bit, although still hard as diamond, and then ... it began to grow. Not in width -- only in length. It was growing out to be seven inches, 10, a whole foot ... and then it kept growing. It was slowly getting longer and longer, the tender pink helmet that was his cockhead staying exactly the same size -- he just now had a shaft that was longer than he was. Michael couldn't explain the feeling but ... it felt weirdly pleasurable. The longer it got, the hornier he got, as if suddenly the extra room allowed him even more of those pleasurable tingles that come when you're harder than you've ever been before. At first, Michael, whose bound bare feet were curling and rolling around in pleasure, wanted it to keep growing, and then, he shuddered: his cock had a bit of a curve to it, and as such, it now several-feet-long manhood was heading for one place and one place only: directly into my hand. Upon realizing what was happening, he began struggling more and more, doing everything he could to loosen the shoelaces that held him in this spread-eagle position on a metallic grid several feet above the black stage floor. Yet nothing could stop his cock's trajectory: it extended out until it was just three inches away from my hand. I could easily grab it if I wanted to, yet abstained. Instead, I just looked at his cockhead looking directly at me, hard as stone, beet red with horniness, dribbling out a faint bit of precum, eager for release. With the bottle of golden liquid still open, I took the hand that wasn't holding the goop-covered cloth and simply poured a bit of this liquid on Michael's tender cockhead -- it instantaneously twitched a bit, rising up a couple inches before returning to its regular height. It liked what it felt, the warm goop moistening his cockhead quite pleasurably. I watched as small drops fell down from the head, his cock again twitching a bit with pleasure. I looked right back up into his terrified eyes.

"Have you ever had your apple polished?"

Before he could respond, I took my cloth covered in goop and wrapped it around his cockhead. Slowly, I twisted it to the left, then slowly twisted it to the right, the moist golden goop acting as a perfect lubricant. It was driving his cockhead insane with pleasure, giving it constant attention yet never enough to produce an orgasm. I just twirled the moist rag one way, then the other, all very casually. One way, then the other, the goop moving and touching every part of his cockhead, cockrim, and tip of his shaft with silky glee. He fucking loved the feeling (nice to see those toes bend and flex as I did this), and then it came: that cock twitch. Instead of rising a few inches though, it remained trapped inside my fabric grip. Oh man, how terrible would that be? To want your cock to twitch but being unable to because I'm holding onto it. I definitely feel your manhood trying to express itself, but nope: just constant moisture motion was all it was getting. Suddenly, Michael knew what it felt like to be at the brink.

"Gaaaah!" he exclaimed as I twisted it once again, swirling those horny tingles inside his cock. How surreal it felt, to be above the ground and for me to be nearly ten feet below him yet still controlling his most intimate of appendages. As I did this, I gave the nod. One of the crewmembers up on the grid has his own bottle of goop, and proceeded to drip it right onto the base of Michael's extra-long cock. He felt it drip down his shaft, a non-stop golden river of mystery liquid that was coating his manhood with moist pleasure, exposing it to the air in the room and letting the air itself excite and tingle him. Before long, the goop that the crew member poured had made its way down to my fabric, and it made for a constant replenishment of lubricant, each slow twist of the cloth in my hand causing Michael to reach a new level of horniness. I didn't even have to look to know that he probably had a good amount of precum mixing in with this goop as I twisted and swirled it around his cockhead and cockrim, his gigantically long cock glistening, reflecting twinkles of the stagelights he himself hung only minutes earlier. The dull fireworks in his loin were going off like the 4th of July. Michael had to cum NOW, but I wasn't going to let him, something that frustrated him all the more when I felt another twitch coming on, but refused to allow it to fly -- all it knew was the heaven and hell of a moist, twisty rag on his manhood, and that's all I *wanted* him to know. I was enjoying watching him go through living hell.

Michael's fevered brain couldn't take it anymore. Its stream-of-conscious thoughts were all about sex, with cock, cum, and orgasm all running a very close second (and naked, oh god, and nipples all running in a tight third).

Then, right underneath his balls, he felt the feather.

A too-soft, ticklish feather stroking his glands, stroking the underside of his balls, and his tender gooch. A crewmember up there was having a lot of fun. At one point he just teased the dangling undercarriages of one ball sac ... then the other ... then back to the first one, twirling and teasing and tickling this whole time, all while mixing with his nipples being flicked and his cockhead being swirled around with liquid pleasure.

The tingles mounted in his balls, in his too-long shaft, in his tip, his orgasm practically registering on the Richter scale. Then he crossed the threshold, he was going to c...

+ + +

"'mon!" He shouted, his body shooting bolt upright at attention. Michael's eyes were wide, his chest absolutely covered in sweat, his lungs panting heavily. Michael got his bearings -- he was in bed and ... oh dear fuck he just had another dream, didn't he? He'd look under the sheets to see if he came or not, but he already knew -- he could feel it under the sheets. An amount of semen this large was just downright humiliating. Michael sighed. He missed the best part, yet again, yet every detail of the dream rang through as vivid as day.

As he got about what was now becoming a regular routine following these dreams -- cleaning his sheets and feeling confused and oddly guilty over the whole thing -- he felt weirdly angry. He knew I had something to do with this, but couldn't figure as to exactly what. Yet my seemingly knowing texts and appearance in the latter two dreams -- all of which featured my own fetishes, not his -- were driving him over the edge. For someone who liked being in control of things, Michael was none too pleased over the notion that someone was controlling his subconscious. He got out his phone and sent off an angry text message to me, reading "Listen, I don't know what you're [sic] game is, but you need to tell me NOW!" He placed the phone on his desk and just stared at it for about two solid minutes, waiting for a response.

Nothing.

Before long, five minutes passed, then ten, then 30. Michael was positive he was going to get the response he needed before too long. He got out his favorite rubber bouncy ball, tossing it in the air and catching it, passing time with repetitive motion as it seemed to help his brain think. Up and down. Up and down. Then, during one attempt at a catch, he dropped it and saw it fall underneath his bed. "Dammit," he muttered aloud. He went and got on his hands and knees and reached as far as he could on his apartment's hardwood floor, reaching for the ball, touching it with the tips of his fingers once, and then getting a grip on it the second time, rolling it back to him. Yet once it was in his paws, he heard something -- a very, very faint chirp. He knew immediately that this wasn't his phone -- he was very familiar with the dying sounds it made when the battery was low -- it was, something altogether different. And very faint as well, as he couldn't hear it again. He stopped all movement, attuned his ears to the air, and ... nothing. Some 30 seconds passed. Nothing. It seemed -- there it was! He heard it again, and it was definitely coming from underneath his bed. He looked and scanned and searched with his eyes, and then, he saw it: just underneath his headboard, a very, very small rectangular chip of some sort. He pulled it off, seeing it was attached by some sort of sticky substance, and examined it closely. For being one as familiar as he was with electronics as he was, he couldn't fathom what this did. There seemed to be some sort of broadcasting element to it, but he was unsure. What did it do? Why was it here? And, more importantly, how did it get there?

Michael had a hell of a gut -- it knew something was up and was right virtually every time. This time, he knew, somehow, that I was responsible for this. Instead of waiting for a text message, he took matters into his own hands, throwing on some socks and shoes and taking his car over to my own apartment. He wasn't driving angry, but he was assuredly driving with purpose.

My door buzzed. I pressed on the intercom, expecting a package from UPS or something.

"Hello?" I asked through the muffled talkbox.

"It's Michael. Open up. Right now."

I could hear him speak with immediate purpose. This was serious. Not one to mess around with such matters, I buzzed him up without questioning him further.

He climbed three flights of stairs surprisingly quickly. He knocked on my door. I opened it up, trying to be as civil as possible.

"Hey there Michael! What brings you to ..."

He spoke pointedly: "You need to sit down, right now."

"Um, can I offer you ..."

"Sit. Now."

I went over to my own ratty couch and sat down. He closed my door behind him, and immediately took control of the situation, walking around as if he lived here and I was the guest. He pulled out the small microchip device and held it up.

"OK, what is this, and what does it do?" he asked.

"Um, well," I squirmed, "it's not really a ... it's hard to describe really ..."

"Well try," he insisted, "and try hard."

Not being completely put in my place, I suddenly went about to being on the sly about things. "Well, Michael, this little baby does something pretty goddamn impressive: it taps into your dreams, and it turns 'em into, well, whatever I want them to be."

"You're fucking lying."

"Really?" I said, standing up. "You probably don't want to admit it but you enjoyed the jungle vine sucking you off. You probably were surprised how much you enjoyed being manipulated on that pool table. Hell, I'm sure you wish your cock was actually that long, having oil dripped on it while feathering your balls ..."

"BUT THEY AREN'T WHAT I WANT!" he shouted.

"Well why did you cum, then?"

A pause filled the air.

"Well ...", he started, struggling for an answer, "I mean, if anyone did that to your ... to your cock or sucked it that way or ... I mean ... who wouldn't cum to that? It's just, ya know ..."

"It was new, which was scary." I calmly explained.

"No, it's not even that, it's just ... why are you forcing your fantasies into my brain?"

There was a pause again. I smiled.

"I think you better sit down, Michael."

A tenuous pause filled the air, and then we both went to the couch and sat down, the playing field a bit more even, the tension somewhat deflated.

"Michael," I started, "I got my fetishes. You know about them, undoubtedly. I also have the strangest feeling that you could care less about them. I mean, a male foot fetish. I'm sure you look at it and wonder what the living hell is attractive about such things, am I right?"

"Well, I mean, I don't want to be cold about it ..." he said very non-judgmentally.

"It's OK, Michael -- I definitely get it. I'm not here trying to 'turn you on' to my own fetishes. That's just ... well, it's not cruel, but having anything forced upon you is wildly unpleasant. I guess I just wanted to share something with you. Something personal."

"Too personal," he interjected.

"Yes, undoubtedly. Yet ... well, you're a sexy guy, Michael."

"Um ... excuse me?"

I looked at him cock-eyed. "Seriously? You're going to play this game?"

"What game?"

"The 'oh, I never thought of myself attractive' gambit? That's *so* beneath you, Michael."

"Hey! It's legit!" he exclaimed.

"Michael, you have some wonderful exes. You have some people that look at you in a mixture of awe and lust. To sit there and think that you aren't at all desirable physically is absurd. I've been wanting to do deliciously terrible things to you for some time, and this was ... well, this was my way of somewhat meeting halfway on the true reality of it."

"Well, I mean ... thank you? I guess?" he stated quixotically.

"Dude, I don't desire you romantically. Get that notion out of your head."

"I mean ... OK."

"I don't want to kiss you."

He tilted his head. "Um, OK."

"All I want to do is just terrible things to you altogether briefly."

"Like what?"

I paused for a second. He asked a question as to what I wanted to do to him. He actually *wanted* to know more. I was very intrigued, yet curious."

"I'm going to take a shot in the dark here and guess that you've never once had your toes sucked on, am I right?"

"Um, that would be a yes," he said non-chalantly, amusing me greatly.

"I have a feeling that you would not believe me for a second if I told you it was a surprisingly fun experience, am I right?"

"Yes."

"Well Michael, here is what I would say to you. Trust me. Trust me one time and one time only. Allow me to try this and add this to your book of WTF-experiences. You have my personal guarantee that you won't regret this."

His eyebrow cocked. "Personal guarantee?"

"Yes."

"And what if I do regret this?"

"I'll give you $100 every month for the rest of your life." Hell, I was surprised that shot out of me as well.

I could see Michael's brain mulling this utterly strange, totally bizarre proposition. His face turned neutral, and then he looked directly at me.

"I literally can't believe I'm doing this," he said, as he started unlacing his shoes. I did everything I could to suppress the biggest smile I've ever had. Both sitting on the couch, he simply swung his legs over so that his socked feet were directly in my lap. "OK," he said, "have at it."

I didn't need to be told twice.

I started be rubbing his arches, explaining along the way: "You see Michael, I'm going to start out very slowly, rubbing your feet and basically getting you to relax. As easy as it would be to jump into things right now, I'm not going to -- it'd be insanely weird for everyone. I just want to ease you into this, slowly." My hands got a bit more of a grip as they rubbed his socked soles, but was feeling resistance from his muscles. "Jesus Christ you're tense."

"You could say that."

"No, Michael, you don't understand: you are fucking *tense*. Like, I'm not sure if you've been massaged ... well, ever!"

"I mean ... yeah, I guess that's a valid point but ... well, yeah."

"Poor guy. Well, I'm not gonna rewrite the wheel here or anything but we'll see if we can at least make some of that go away."

"Heh, 'rewrite the wheel'," he scoffed.

"Hey, shut up! I'm concentrating!" It was nice to joke even at a time like this.

I massaged his tense feet for a good ten minutes before I finally felt them relax, the toes becoming more amendable to me moving them, his arches no longer giving his tendons a constant workout. Once he was set, I slowly hooked my finger around the rim of his right sock, and slowly, slowly peeled it off his gloriously pale pedal.

"You're enjoying this slow reveal, aren't you?" he commented.

"Michael, it's a foot fetish. Of course I do. There's something that's just so ... weirdly intimate about seeing another guy's toes." The sock was now off, and I was doing the same to his other foot.

"Is it the shape of them or what?" he inquired, seemingly curious.

"Well, yeah. I mean ... it's hard to articulate. It's half of what they look like and half of what they represent. I mean ... I dunno, it's strange."

"How about the smell?"

"Shit," I said disarmingly, "That's the best part."

"Really?"

"Oh my god yes. With most sexual interactions, smell is one of the single most important sensations. That whiff of perfume, that post-coital sweat, you name it -- it's astonishing."

"So, a used pair of socks to you is ... ?"

"Heaven."

"Ah," he said.

"But, ya know, not too rank," I clarified. "A man has his limits."

"I am learning so many things tonight," he said jokingly. I had no idea as to why he was in such a jovial mood about the whole thing, but I definitely was going to take it.

I arched my head around and sniffed the base of his bare toes, and the feeling left me positively radiating horniness. He certainly may not have understood the appeal, but I had come across the sweet spot. Testing the limits of things, I extended my tongue just a bit and licked the base of his toes. He pulled back a bit.

"Gah!" he exclaimed. "That tickles!"

"Your feet are ticklish? I wouldn't have guessed that." I noted, pretending, again, to be extremely matter-of-factual about such a tantalizing revelation.

"Well, they are."

"OK," I said, "I'll be very gentle then ..."

With that, I continued to lightly tongue his exposed footflesh, but very slowly so that he knew where the tongue was going next. I started slithering my moist tongue in-between his toes, bits of saliva running down as I went, and he did everything he could to suppress his laughter: even with me being careful as hell, it still tickled him. His smile was huge, and he was so obviously trying to make sure it didn't go beyond a smile, the tickles definitely mounting an attack at bay. I went from one toe-slot to another, leaving his toenails positively glistening by the end. One toe to another, that warm, moist slithering thing rounding up tickles he didn't even know existed and sending them straight through his body. He was simultaneously loving and hating it. I, however, was just loving it.

After about ten more minutes, I was done, and his feet were coated in horny saliva. He brought his legs in and wrapped his arms around his knees, leaving his bare feet flat on the couch cushion. I thought it was a goddamn hot pose myself. I looked at his face -- he may not have enjoyed it, but I could tell he definitely didn't hate it. The laughter was still very much at bay.

"So," I started, half-jokingly, "should I grab my checkbook?"

In his eyes, he truly was weighing a decision. However, his half-smile never fully receded. I could tell I was safe.

"You know what, let's call this a favor to you. You're good," he said as he started putting his socks back on.

"Strange?" I inquired.

"Definitely."

"One for your book of memories?"

"Assuredly," he said as he now started putting on and lacing his shoes.

"Enjoyable?"

That one hung in the air for a bit.

"I'll get back to you on that," he said, his tone surprisingly earnest.

"Well, Michael, as my favor to you, I'll never mention this night to anyone."

"Thank you." He was getting ready to leave.

"So we good?" I asked, actually wanting to know.

"... yeah. Yeah. We're good." he said, reassuring himself almost as much as he did me.

"Well drive safe. We'll talk soon."

"Yeah. Later." And with that, he left. I personally couldn't believe how positively the evening ended. Even with him storming in here, he didn't ask question as to how I even got this wonderful chip which locked onto REM brainwave frequencies and interjected waves of its own, much less how it worked (hell, I couldn't even explain all of that). He didn't ask as to how I got it under his bed or even how long it had been there. He only wanted certain things from me, and got a whole lot more -- probably more than he bargained for. Either way, given everything leading up to it, I was amazed by how well things went.

Driving home, Michael kept running through the events in his head. Even with everything, he could tell I wasn't being malicious to him -- I was just trying a very unusual way to reach out to him. He could very well have been pissed as hell and he'd be justified: this was an invasion of privacy on an unfathomable scale. Yet, deep down, he still wanted this friendship to work. He let things go, he forgave, he moved on. Even as he pressed down on the pedal to accelerate after a red light, he could feel my saliva still drying in-between his toes. He wouldn't necessarily call it a bad sensation, but it was certainly, well, unique in his mind.

That night, he got to bed, and his nerves were calmed. He was at ease, sure that nothing insane was going to happen tonight. As such, the second his head hit his pillow, he knew things were going to turn out alright.

What surprised him, however, was that even without a device feeding him information, I still appeared in his dreams that night ...

ONE FINGER

$+++$

Those who know me well know I have a fairly unspoken rule with my fetish: I'm really, really not into older guys. I'm only interested in guys right around my age. This isn't a personal thing or a vendetta thing -- it's just how my brain works. I have definitely made exceptions before (hi there, Fing!), and they've all been wonderful, but the truth of the matter is, it's not my bag. However, as is often the case with my stories, I'm extremely fascinated with the destruction of the male ego in its various forms, particularly when the brash meets its match. The story I had in mind for "One Finger" had been generated for awhile, but once I met a nice tan-skinned hot-shot who was the talk of the town here in real life, I knew I had a pretty fun avatar to play with. The cocky got its say, certainly, but before long, it ran into experience: cold, hard hard experience without any artifice, any need for extended games or (ugh) drama. The characters presented here were meant to meet, because when the cocky kid thinks he knows all, dishing out smarmy dismissals of those whom he's sure he's pegged on first pigeonholed assumption, it's up to someone to knock him back into place, and getting to do so here in this story was all sorts of rewarding. You agree with me, don't ya?

"Oh fuck ... oh FUCK!"

Angelo looked on, smiling, his hand slowly working the cock of the hipster boy that lay naked beside him. The boy's head tilted back, unable to take in the rush of ecstasy his body was experiencing as Angelo worked the swollen, trembling cock like a pro, the side of his index finger rubbing back and forth over the lip of the boy's cockhead, the motion made all the more frictionless by the copious amounts of sticky-moist precum that were flooding from his member. The brown-haired boy with the ten-o-clock shadow had never been worked so good, and before long, a full-grown lust monster took over, and the boy shouted desperately: "Yes ... YES! FUCCCCK YESSS!" And with that, rockets of sperm fired out of him, getting in his chair, then his face, and then down to his chest and stomach as they decreased in intensity. His panting was almost as loud as his orgasmic cries, sweat appearing everywhere on his skin. His heavy breathing slowly turned into normal breaths, but his very spirit wouldn't be so lucky, that orgasm having shattered just about every notion he ever had about pleasure. He reached around for his glasses on his night stand, and when he put them on, he saw his young Latino friend getting ready to leave.

"Oh -- hey!" he shouted, almost desperate, all while suddenly feeling weirdly embarrassed that he was naked. "Where are you going? What's ... what's going on?"

"I'm leaving," Angelo said, a leather jacket covering his bare chest and he finished buttoning up his tight black pants.

"But I ... I mean ..."

Angelo shot a glance to his latest conquest. "What, you want me to stay?"

"Yeah, I mean, especially after something like that, it just makes sense that ..."

"What? We kiss? I hear about your secret fantasies of boning one of the guys from Arcade Flames?"

"Arcade Fire, actually."

"Whatever. I mean, what do you think tonight was, boy?'

The lightly bearded collegiate lad looked around for the words he was trying to think of, slightly hurt. "I just thought that tonight -- as random as it was -- " (Angelo rolled his eyes to that) "was the start of something. Maybe something special, even."

Angelo took a heavy breath and a stern face. "Listen, I'm going to say this only once, and I don't care how hard it hurts: you're gay, honey. I know that's not what you tell your girlfriend, but judging by how you still have cum in your excuse for a beard, her mouth could never do what my hand just did. You're going to deny that you enjoyed this for weeks, maybe even months, and you're going to think that what we had was special. As you keep looking out for more guys to blow you and fuck you and turn you inside out, you'll realize that while women look for love, gay guys are looking for an honest fuck, without strings and without whatever you're about to say to me after I'm done speaking."

Visibly shaken, the boy struggled to make sense of what was being said to him: "I just thought ... I mean, I just thought that ..."

Angelo held his finger in the air: "I'm gonna stop you right there before I get bored. Drop it, move on, and whatever." Angelo walked out the room and walked down the hallway of whatever dorm he was invited into no more than 90 minutes ago. Right as he was about to leave, he heard the boy's voice calling from way down in the hall. Angelo didn't even want to turn around, but did so, seeing the pathetic newbie chasing after him in boxers with precum stains in the front, showing just how bad a boner he had earlier.

"Hey -- come back!"

"Leaving," Angelo said, turning and exiting once and for all.

"Will I ever see you again?" the hipster boy shouted.

"I'd worry about the cum in your hair first," quipped Angelo as the door shut behind him, leaving the boy all dejected and sad. Shame too -- Angelo really liked this one.

+ + +

An hour later, Angelo was at Swing, the local gay bar in town, sucking down another bottled beer, his eye darting around the room, lazily: nothing intrigued him. He recognized all the types: the recently-liberated jock boy reveling in his newfound status as a hunky sex god, the introverted goth types who didn't just fuck -- they practically worshiped the chance to suck a cock for way longer than necessary, and (of course) the guys over 35 who Angelo couldn't give less of a fuck about. He took another sip of his beer even though he knew he'd have to work out a bit more in the morning so not to reshape his already-sightly abs. Starting to feel buzzed, his eyes drew upward, staring at the lights above and how, despite his hundreds of visits here, he never noticed how perpetually dim they were. Was it mood lighting? Was it supposed to be (gag) romantic? What a weird setting, he thought. He took another sip, catching glimpses of "rubbers" (guys he fucked once and then effectively "thew away") and his regulars who became less and less interesting as time bore on. Angelo, once again, was bored.

He started thinking that perhaps it'd be more fun to go home, put in some poppers, and jack off to whatever was new on Xtube while making remarkably explicit Casual Encounters posts on Craigslist when he noticed someone sitting by himself in of the booths in the corner of the bar. This man was definitely older -- at least 40 judging by what he could make out in the soft-hued corners of this rainbow-colored watering hole -- but he was ... staring right at Angelo. Right at him. Like a target. Angelo's head tilted back a bit in disbelief, but the man's gaze didn't flinch, instead taking a steady sip of his own beer. Angelo would normally tease older guys like that by saying "Pervert!" in passing, knowing it'd piss them off, but something was profoundly different about this guy. The look he was giving him wasn't one of carnal lust or curiosity -- it was just ... knowing. That alcoholic buzz now officially reaching cruising altitude, Angelo thought "Why the fuck not?" He set his beer down and walked on over to the man's booth. As he approached, the man adopted a slight smile, but it was very faint, very controlled. Angelo stood at the edge of the man's table, striking a pose, almost.

"So what -- you like what you see?" teased the tipsy Latino boy.

"It's suitable," the man said, taking another sip of his beer. Angelo eyed his features more closely: thin glasses, his hair already graying a bit, his teal polo shirt assuredly showing a man who was not in "the scene" much at all. Still, the comment stung Angelo a bit. For a man who was lusted after by both gay men and straight women, this was the first time he could ever remember someone not falling for his spell right away.

"Suitable?" Angelo quipped, his voice drenched in sarcasm, "I'm sorry, did they you run out of *Women of Wal-Mart* DVDs recently? That more your speed?"

"Not really, much as how 'bitchy queen' isn't your default setting either. In fact, it's not even a setting for you -- it's a pose."

"A pose?"

"Yeah -- it's a lot more fun being dismissive than it is being dismissed, isn't it?"

Defiant, Angelo said "Um, I've never been dismissed from anything, honey."

"And therein lies your problem," said the man, taking another sip from his beer, casually.

"What?" said Angelo, who would be in a huff if he wasn't so confused.

"Sit down, boy."

Angelo didn't take too well to direct commands, but there was something about the cadence in this man's voice that compelled him to figure out what this man's deal was. Angelo quietly slid into the opposite side of the booth, wondering what was about to happen.

"So, why is it bad that I've never been dismissed from anything?"

"'cos it's boring," said the man.

"How could a never-ending plethora of chocolates ever be boring?" asked Angelo, pleased with his choice of analogies.

"'cos it's repetitious. Because you can have fuck after fuck after fuck, but what's really so good about that? I'm guessing that most of them are pretty average, right? Every once in awhile you find one that's half-way good, and you reward that boy with what? A date? One of your patented handjobs? Please. When was the last truly good orgasm you had?"

"Well, last week, I was playing around with this exchange student ..."

"No, that's not what I'm talking about," the man interrupted. "I'm not talking about the last really fun one you had, or even the last repeat visit you had. I assume you blew that heteroflexible boy you met earlier?"

"Who?" said Angelo, genuinely not aware of who he was talking about.

"The one in the Arcade Fire T-shirt."

"Oh, him. No, I just gave him a handjob."

"And how did he react?" the man asked.

"Heh, it was like he saw the stars for the very first time."

"And when was the last time someone made you see the stars?"

Angelo paused. On one hand, all he could do was wonder what the fuck this guy was getting at. On the other hand, he was somewhat stumped by that last exchange. Not one to show signs of weakness however, his bitchy queen started up again:

"You know, I don't take advice from guys who should be in the old folks home. Your time has come and gone."

"As has yours."

"EXCUSE ME?" Angelo shot back, vain and defiant.

"Yeah, boy. I've seen you here for a few nights now, and I've seen you try every flavor of man that there is in this bar. You're insatiable, and for that very reason, you're unsatisfied. You think you know so much about the scene but the truth is you're bored as hell, and that's largely because you're boring. Your primary function in life right now is to fuck and be fucked, and somehow after each climax you think, briefly, that you're happy. And then you go home to your bed, still alone, unfulfilled, downloading porn illegally because gay men have suffered for dozens of years so why shouldn't you get a well-made fisting video for free, right? You've been unhappy for years and you convince yourself otherwise and you don't fuck guys over how old: 30? 28?"

"35, actually." Angelo said, a bit flabbergasted.

"That sounds about right. It's a lot more fun to have playthings than it is to have experience or even meet someone who would know what to do with you but that invisible tiara you place upon your own head is ready to slip at any moment. You can sling as many snarky remarks as you want with me but I can clearly see that you're the shaken one, and however clever you think you are, I've heard whatever you're going to say a hundred times over, so you might as save it.'

Angelo's mouth parted, words ready to come out, but nothing did. Half-words almost formed, but the traffic-jam of information that hit his brain was just too much for him to handle. He wasn't sure if he was angry or apologetic or pissed or excited or what. After a minute of sputtering out barely-there syllables, Angelo finally said something coherent:

"So ... what ... do you want with me?"

The man grinned, and took his final swig of his beer. "I want to show you what you're missing.'

"And what, pray tell, am I missing?"

"I'm going to make you beg to cum with nothing but a finger, boy."

"Um, for your information, I've been fingerbanged before, old man," he said.

"Oh I know, boy," the older man said, getting up, "and what I want to do is nothing even remotely like it." He then leaned in and whispered into Angelo's ear: "I'm going to break you like a wild stallion, and you're going to love it."

The man, now standing, pulled out his wallet, and produced a business card from it. He handed it to Angelo and began speaking as he walked towards the front doors of the bar: "Be there, tomorrow. 7PM."

"Not tonight?" Angelo said, almost pleading.

"You're drunk."

Stunned by how blunt this man was, Angelo just froze there for a moment. Right as the man was leaving, in a moment of desperation, Angelo took a few steps towards him and shouted "My name's Angelo, by the way!"

"I don't care," the man said as the door closed behind him, not even looking back for a half-second.

Angelo didn't know what hit him: he sounded ... desperate. "My name's Angelo, by the way!" Who the fuck says that? He knew exactly who said that: first-timers, rubbers, desperate scenesters. What the hell made him say that? What took over? He was so mad at himself right now. He looked down at the card in his hands, and it had an address that appeared to be just outside of downtown. A building filled with studio apartments if he wasn't mistaken. Despite his curiosity, Angelo made a solemn promise to himself: he would not show up at this man's apartment no matter what.

+ + +

Knocking on the door of the man's apartment, Angelo, strangely, felt nervous. His pants were the same from last night but this time around he wore just a form-fitting black T-shirt and put a little more product in his hair. He never felt this nervous about a meet before, but then again, this was the first time he was really at someone else's mercy.

There was no answer, no sound of movement, even, coming from the other side of the of the door on this building's large third floor. Angelo knocked again. He heard the echoes of each rapt sound bounce against the walls of an apartment that sounded very spacious. He stood there, waiting, impatient, and was about to walk away when the door opened and the man greeted him.

"Come on in," the man said, with a smile.

Angelo did, and the site was a dream come true: spacious and minimal, this massive abode had dark hardwood floors, kitchen counters made of white tile, and an island fireplace. It was incredible. The couches were also white, but aside from a few magazines on the coffee tables, there wasn't much in terms of decorations. There were a few bookshelves -- all filled with books that appeared well-worn -- a vinyl player, a large plasma TV against the wall, and a few art-deco paintings, but overall, the aesthetic was pretty direct. There were large wall-sized windows that allowed a small outlook over the city as well, which made Angelo feel like he was in some sort of movie. As he looked around in total awe, he failed to notice that the man had walked up right next to him with two glasses of white wine -- one for him, one for his guest.

"Please," he said, kindly placing the long-stem in Angelo's hand. He extended his own glass out for a toast: "to our health," which Angelo clinked to without even thinking before taking a sip of the luxurious liquid.

"So," Angelo started, "how strong is the roofie you mixed into this?"

The man scoffed, smiling. "Oh please: roofies are used by guys who don't have a real shot at anything." Angelo laughed at that comment, largely because he agreed.

The guys made small talk while staring out the window onto the dusk-lit city below. It was actually kind of pleasant. Once the guys were done with their glasses, however, the man set them on his kitchen counter and then gestured with his fingers to Angelo, saying "Come with me."

Angelo followed and the man lead Angelo to another room in his studio, and in it, there was a simple wooden structure which housed -- a slightly above-ground-level sex swing. There was a small white credenza next to it, but seeing the sling was all Angelo needed to scoff.

"Really?" he said, turning to the man. "That's it? A sling?"

The man smiled again. "When was the last time you trusted someone wholesale, boy?"

"My name's Angelo."

"Again, I don't care, boy," the man said rather bluntly. "When was the last time you really trusted someone without question?"

"I'd say ... never," said Angelo, a bit of fire coming back to his words.

"Then trust me this one time," the man said, the proposition hanging in the air. Given that Angelo's take so far of this older gent was that he knew what he was doing every step of the way, he said something that he only previously said in desperation: "Why not?"

The man instructed Angelo to strip down to his boxers and socks and nothing else. (Angelo made some cocky remark about why the man didn't want to see his "massive" member, but the man cut him down to size simply by saying "Whatever you're about to show me, trust me: I've seen bigger.") Instead of getting in the sling so that he was face up, the man strapped Angelo into the sling so that he was actually face down. Instead of being a relaxed, reclining position, he was at somewhat of a 45-degree angle, belly out, his whole body sagging from his arms, as if his ribcage was a pinata of some sort, just sagging there while his arms and legs held up the weight. There was a bit of a strain (of course) but it wasn't anything Angelo couldn't handle. Angelo tried moving around, but with his arms and legs stretched out at the angles they were, he couldn't do much in the way of escaping anything that came into his personal bubble.

"Snug?" the man asked as he adjusted one last strap.

"Yeah. I've been tied up worse," noted Angelo, thinking casual mentions of his own experiences might impress the man. The man looked at Angelo and then looked away, not even as much acknowledging the comment in question. Out of the corner of his eye, Angelo could spot the man grabbing something from a table that was set up nearby, and as he walked closer to Angelo, the boy could see what it was but only before it was too late: an incredibly sturdy leather blindfold. Without even asking, the man placed it over Angelo's eyes, adjusting the strap behind his head, brushing some of Angelo's jet-black hair out of the way as he did so. The man wasn't playing around or even taking in moments for himself as he fixed the strap tightly around Angelo's scalp, no: he was all about efficiency, which Angelo wouldn't admit frightened him just a little bit.

Angelo's vision was pitch black. The inside of the leather mask had these soft pouchy bumps that fit snugly into his eye-sockets -- he couldn't even open his eyelids if he wanted to, but he wasn't necessarily uncomfortable either. The man was truly limiting the boy's senses. Angelo could hear the sound of a wooden chair being pulled up in front of the boy. Angelo's body was tense, as all it was doing was simply swaying ever so slightly in the dead air of the room. He literally had no idea what was about to happen next.

Some 30 seconds or so passed. Then 30 seconds more. Then a minute. "Um, you going to do anything?" asked Angelo in a tone that simply oozed sarcasm. Nothing. Not even the creaking sound of the man adjusting himself in the wooden chair. Just, silence. As time pressed on, Angelo felt his body subconsciously tense up more and more, growing ever-fearful of what was being planned. The more tense he got, the more desperate the scenarios in his head spiraled, a rare tinge of doubt creeping in to his mind, thinking that perhaps he is actually in the clutches of a conniving serial killer or someone who wants to turn him into a full blown leather boy or was hired to do a number on him after he dumped some guy cold blooded-ly ("That's a word, right?" Angelo thought) ...

And that's when Angelo quickly shuddered "*Oh God*!", his body spasming. On his left nipple, he suddenly felt this chill, cool cream get applied. A huge gob of it too. It must be ... moisturizer ... that had been refrigerated That was the only thing it could be. And now, it was hanging from his nipples and boy was it a shock to the system. Even with his black ankle socks still on, Angelo could feel the chill all the way down to his toes. Then, with almost the same level of surprise, a gob of the cool cream was placed on his right nipple. It wasn't five seconds before he felt both his nips jutting out at full attention. Already he could feel those dirty, dark tingles start to form at the base of cock, but there was no immediate movement. For now, it was all chill sensation.

"Now," started the man, his voice cutting through the silent air with authority and volume, "What was the deal we made last night, boy?"

"Ohhhhh," Angelo shuddered, his body still adjusting to its new nip-temp, "we ... we no you were going to ... ohhhh ... get me off."

"Nope, that wasn't the deal."

"You're lying then! You said ..."

"I said I was going to get you off with a finger, boy. And that's exactly what I'm going to do."

"Well," started Angelo, sounding like he was on the verge of another gasp of pleasure, "isn't the moisturizer cheating?"

"Not really," said the man, "as the only other liquids I need are going to come from you."

Angelo was almost scared, but that didn't last for long: the man's index finger was suddenly inside his Angelo's helpless bellybutton. The boy yelped. Even though he couldn't see it, Angelo felt as if he somehow knew the man was smiling right now.

At first, the well-manicured finger just stayed there in Angelo's bellybutton, but very slowly, it began to wiggle a bit, twisting around inside Angelo's sensitive tummyhole. A few boyish giggles bled out of Angelo's mouth. "Hehe -- stop it! Stop! That tickles!"

"I know," the man said, coldly.

The finger wormed its way around, the wiggling slowly and steadily growing intensity. It scratched the sensitive inside of the boy's button, but each little scrape of his fingernail unearthed a few more tickles than the last scratch. Over and over again, scratchy scratchy scratchy, tickle tickle tickle. Angelo's arms strained and flexed to try and get his body away from the wiggling finger, but nothing could be done: the finger was in there too deep, and it was tickling like its life depended on it.

Just when Angelo couldn't take it anymore, the finger removed itself from Angelo's belly button. A minute passed, and already, Angelo could feel sweat forming on his body. Then, out of nowhere, he felt the finger fondle his left earlobe a bit. "Hey, cut that out!" Angelo said, once again in a boyish fashion that surprised even himself. Yet the finger wasn't happy with his head movements. It went out to fondle that earlobe again, softly, before tracing behind his ear a bit, then playfully poking a bit on the inside. "Stop it!" shouted Angelo, through laughter, but the constant exploration of the finger wasn't stopping. The finger's favorite thing to do right now seemed to be lightly flicking the lobe back and forth before exploring the ins and outs of the ear itself, poking around like a miniature bloodhound's nose, not caring where it ends up. All of this playfulness was still getting Angelo to laugh. The finger then went around to the other ear and did the same thing, fondling and fondling the ear like it was its own precious, ticklish thing. Angelo couldn't remember the last time someone was this playful, but for whatever reason, those tingles in his loins continued to mount because of it.

The finger then began tracing along the smooth sides of the boy's neck, but one it began running underneath Angelo's chin, he lost it. "Ahaha get out of there!" he screamed as he did everything he could to bring his chin inward, but it was to no avail: the finger could travel wherever it wanted to, but playing with the boy's sensitive chin was actually tickling him.

"I got you by the hair of your chiny chin chin," the man said, glee in his voice as he played with his toy. The childish talk, for whatever reason, was really getting to Angelo. After all, he was often the dominant force in all of his scenarios, so for someone else to be taking the reigns, much less treating him like a helpless child, was only adding on to the psychological torment, as if each degrading phrase somehow increased the boy's ticklishness. Tickle tickle went the finger, and no matter what awkward position Angelo put his face in, the finger somehow was able to scratch somewhere new and exposed at a second's notice and conjure even more tickles out of the boy.

Without warning, the finger left Angelo's chin and then dived right into the little mountain of moisturizer on the boy's left peck and began fondling the pointy nip tip with absolute relish. Angelo screamed, his body lurched to one side, but soon came back into position, the finger circling the sensitive circle of pink flesh as the base of his nipple, then tracing up the protruding center and then down the other side, doing this over and over again, sometimes wiggling around on the very tip for a few seconds just to see what kind of reaction it would get, before flicking the pointy mound a bit before circling it again. It was just constant nerve-ending stimulation. When the finger jumped over to the right nipple, Angelo felt a wave of erotic electricity simply surge through his body, feeling it all the way out at the edge of his fingertips. His body flexed and almost leaned into it against his better wishes, almost asking for the nip to be played with all the more. Angelo couldn't believe it, but he felt as if his nipple was almost trying to grow larger. It loved being played with, tormented, fondled. In the back of his mind, he somewhat wished that the man had promised to get him off with at least two fingers.

The finger stopped its devious torment. "You had enough yet?" asked the man. Angelo, panting a bit, said, "What ... what do you think you're doing?'

Without even answering, a fingernail scratched one of Angelo's ribs no his right side. The boy let out a laugh. It poked and wiggled again, although this time a few ribs lower. Then it started scratching the side of his tummy. Angelo, ticklish as all fuckout, clenched his teeth together, defiant to laughter, but the finger wasn't having any of that. It jumped over to his left rips, wiggled there. Then the right ribs. Then the top of his right ribs. Then it traced a left rib back all the way to Angelo's sagging spine. Then the finger just began wiggling and poking wherever it pleased, finding great joy in the deep-seated laughs that could be found by scratching right in-between Angelo's ribs.

Angelo fucking hated this. His teeth were practically grinding against each other to fight off the laughter, but the fingers were too good, poking him in his vulnerable areas, scratching his sexy, sweaty skin, sometimes even working its way up into his hairy armpit, diving into the fleshy center and unearthing metric ton's worth of evil, evil tickles. Right now, the finger was doing serious tickle damage to his left armpit, twisting the hairs around before prodding and poking the center once more, and finally, at the very edge of sanity, Angelo lost it:

"HA HA HA FUCK DEAR FUCK THAT TICKLES PLEASE HA STOPHA!"

It was music to the man's ears.

Now that Pandora's box of laughter was cracked wide open, the finger grew ferocious: the armpits were now being prodded aggressively, a few new nip-flips were thrown in, and those terribly effective between-rib pokes all shot Angelo into a new stratosphere of sexual torment. He was almost dizzy, spending more time exhaling laughs than he was inhaling air, his brain and body now switched over to tickle-input mode and having little time to process anything else. Angelo was getting lost in this stratosphere of half-consciousness ...

... but a single swipe of his cock was all it took to ground him again.

So distracted by his futile attempts to contain his own maniacal laughter, Angelo failed to notice that he was sporting a massive boner through his underwear, and it was already dripping a bit of precum. The finger's smooth run against his shaft was almost like a slap in the face: it almost made him sober up. Before he could even realize it, a pair scissors was cutting off his underwear rather quickly, and before long, Angelo was naked in midair save for his socks. His large, fat cock flopped out, the air of the room surrounding his sweaty balls, giving him a sigh of relief after being cooped up in that underwear for so long. Angelo could sense the man moving, getting behind him, which honestly scared Angelo a bit.

Without warning (as always), the finger dove right into the middle of Angelo's gooch, that too-sensitive fleshy patch between his ass and his scrotum, wiggling and scratching and teasing away. The shock of the sensation made a high-pitch shock-laugh fire out of the boy's esophagus, all before desperate pleas of "No! Pleeeease stop!" followed, mixing in with reticent moans. The finger sometimes strayed and began slowly tracing the gooch down to the underside of the boy's balls, hanging there, exposed.

"I hope, for your sake," started the man, "that your balls aren't ticklish."

For the next hour, the finger teased and traced every curve and crevice of the young man's nutsack, sometimes touching the very bottoms of the balls ever-so-softly, sometimes wiggling their way up the glands that connected to the base of his shaft, sometimes wiggling in-between the two balls just to see if that cause Angelo to emit some sexy little laughs (they did). Dear fuck this finger was having a love affair with the boy's balls. After about 20 minutes of non-stop stimulation, Antonio discovered that, in fact, it was tickling behind the balls that got him the most, as that area was just so damn sensitive. Angelo had been naked in front of guys dozens of times before, but when the barely-touched back of his balls were teased like that, he felt something he had never felt before: vulnerable. Fully, 100% vulnerable. This man was controlling his eager, throbbing cock like a ticklish puppet, each wiggle and light fingernail scrape causing his member to throb or twitch or lift upward on its own, the tingles accumulating in his beet-red cockhead. By the end of that hour of non-stop ball teasing, not only was precum leaking out of the Latino lad, but it had formed a straight, uninterrupted line of the clear manjuice that went from his cock to the floor, where it was beginning to pool. Angelo, truly had never been more horny in his life.

The ball-teasing stopped and not a moment too soon. Every once in awhile, Angelo's blindfolded head would whip around, trying to shake off the constant threat of horny explosion that was forming in his skull. He sensed the man moving around, moving in front of him, and somewhat underneath him. The finger reached up and took a swipe of moisturizer of the boy's right nipple, and then rubbed that moisturizer right in-between where Angelo's cockhead the front of the shaft met. The finger slowly worked the moisturizer in, not focusing on any other area aside from that pinnacle of sensitivity. Stroke. Angelo took in a breath. Stroke. Angelo gasped a little. Stroke. Angelo felt his balls shudder just a bit, but not enough where anything was about to happen.

Then nothing.

Angelo's cock was practically begging for release, his entire shaft having turned as red as his helmet, the whole thing ready to burst if as much as a light breeze rolled through the room. In the back of his mind, Angelo was simply begging for a nipple fondle. Or a rib poke. Or maybe, oh please, a ball fondling? Please? That's all it'd need ...

"Do you want to cum, boy?"

"Fuuuuuck yes," Angelo said, sighing, desperately, defeated.

"OK," said the man, "but only under one condition."

"Yes, please, anything." Angelo was eager to get this over with.

"Once you cum, I get to play with you for as long as I want, no matter how much you beg me to stop."

"FINE!" Angelo screamed. "Just Make. Me. Cum!"

"Your wish," said the man, ever so sly.

He walked behind Angelo, kneeling in-between his suspended legs, and the finger did what it knew the boy liked best: it lightly scratch-tickled the backs of his balls. "Tickle tickle tickle," the man said, teasingly.

He lost it.

In one surge, Angelo felt his cock jut out, rocketing out a cum shot that was as intense as anything he ever felt. Instantly, tingles overtook every square inch of his body. The man's hand suddenly reached around to the shaft and the fingers wrapped around it. It began jerking the boy off mid shoot. The second shot felt about equidistant to the first, the sheer velocity of it making Angelo feel like he was swinging backwards. The hand, especially the the soft side of the index finger, began rubbing back and forth over that sensitive lip of the cockhead, the one that connected with the front of his shaft where the moisturizer was applied earlier. Except now that the moisturizer was worked in, that lip took on a bit of a rubbery feeling, and being stimulated while he was cumming was a sensitivity nightmare. The man's hand continued to jerk furiously as each shot of piping-hot cum came out, and as the pleasure shots died in intensity, the hand kept jerking. Slowly, the lightning bolt of pleasure that was Angelo's cock was becoming more and more a no-touch zone. His sensitivity was through the roof. The tipping point was crossed, and the boy began squirming.

"Please," Angelo said, "please stop!"

"That wasn't the agreement boy," said the man sternly.

"No, please, ha ha this is just ... he he too sensitive!"

"I know."

"No, really!" shouted Angelo. "I'm too sensitive!"

"I know."

"STOP!" he screamed, his body fidgeting with whatever remaining energy it had left.

"No," said the man, watching as the blindfolded boy's next thoughts were drowned out by his own helpless laughter.

The sensitivity jerking was actually tickling poor Angelo, and now his mind was lost in a world where "tickle" was the only word it knew.

+++

Angelo's torment lasted for three more hours. He passed out by the end.

+++

Angelo was once again sipping a beer in Swing, his leather jacket on, unzipped, with no shirt underneath, as per always. Angelo was looking around, looking for new meat, but right now, even the rubbers he once disposed of so fecklessly were now intriguing to him. That night with the man (whose name he never caught) was life-changing. For the first time in his life, he was at someone's complete and utter mercy, and the overwhelming desperate intensity rearranged a lot of things in his brain. He realized that even with his hundreds of experiences, there was still much to learn, and new lessons could come from any place. Angelo put the moratorium on his "over 35" rule for now. He'd take anyone who seems to know what they're doing. In fact, right now, he was ...

"Hey there, Angelo!"

Angelo turned around. It was that hipster boy from a few weeks ago. He was wearing a red flannel shirt that made him look like a lumberjack, but ... something was different about him. He had a confidence to him.

"Um, hey there," Angelo said, unsure of how to react.

"How are you man?" Dear gods this boy was excitable.

"Um, I'm good. How ... how are you?"

"Listen," the boy started. "I wanted to apologize for, um ... our last encounter. I'm sure I seemed desperate and pathetic to you, but that's only because, well, I was. It's ..."

"Stop right there," started Angelo, "don't even say another--"

"No no, let me finish!" the boy said, eager. "A lot of those things you said were ... very true. Very cold, hard truths that I had really ..."

"No," Angelo said, softly. "They weren't."

The hipster boy paused and cocked his head, curious. "What?"

"I was wrong to try and demean you like that," started Angelo, sounding more sage-like than he ever had before. "You're new to the scene, you're young, and a lot of the things I said were reactionary. I was playing the role of the stuck-up queen and I was playing it well. It was wrong to say those things to you."

The boy looked at Angelo, confused. "I ... those things were life-changing. I promise to never be like that again."

Angelo put his beer down, got off his barstool, and grabbed the front of the boy's shirt and pulled him close. "I don't want you to act like a stereotype, boy. I want you to act like you." He pulled him in for a deep kiss, and the hipster boy didn't know what to do, but somewhat leaned into it.

Their lips unlocked. They now stood facing each other, Angelo smirking a bit, which in turn caused the other boy to do the same. Angelo smiled as he spoke: "Tonight, I'm going to change your life boy."

And hours later, he did.

THE LETTER

+ + +

There's loving your fetish, and there's loving your fetish when you're absolutely stoned out of your mind. I'm not an everyday pot user (I gots ta work, kiddos), but the times when I do, I really go for it, getting so high you become stupid, wherein your horniness absolutely takes over and destroys any remnant of rational thought you may have. The orgasms that can be reached are nothing short of transcendent, but I'll be first to admit I've done some stupid things while intoxicated, as we all do: sending out the occasional TMI text message, writing up the too-revealing email that was never meant to be sent, etc. Chuck Klosterman had a great line about this: what aggravated him about writing drunk emails to girls he shouldn't be contacting in the first place wasn't the fact that what he had written was false or untrue; in fact, to the contrary, what he had written hit way too close to home, revealing darker truths he never wanted to. I have a good portion of insanely horny, wildly illogical ramblings stored in email draft folders and various Word docs that will never see the light of day -- the "recipients" that are intended assuredly never, ever, ever need to see them. However, what if one slipped out? What would happen? How utterly, desperately humiliating would it be? When exploring other galaxies with my brain one night, I came up with this idea that -- at the time -- seemed hotter than all get out: to actually <u>be</u> the sandals of your most sought-after foot fetish obsession. To be pressed against his warm feet every day, to feel those toes wiggling around on top of you -- nothing short of foot fetish heaven, am I right? Thus, there seemed no better time to write a quickie such as this, going into all sort of detail about such delirious (and devilishly delicious) idea ...

His cock was throbbing through his jeans, delirious with horny thoughts. After all, Kevin had already had several beers that night -- all while attending a light social occasion with some friends earlier in the evening, although even coming home he didn't feel like he sobered up in the least -- but when he got through his front door, buzzed like a honeybee, he just felt his horny thoughts take over. They dominated every neural pathway and thought. Willingly and with a smile on his face, he submitted to his own naughty fetishes, and they completely dominated him in return.

Kevin sat at his computer, a new beer freshly popped open, checking his bookmarked list of gay foot and tickle blogs, his dick no doubt happy to see many of them were updated. Videos, pics, a cavalcade of candid barefoot and and sandaled photos: it was just nothing but a buffet spread of heavenly delights. Kevin began rubbing his hardening cock through his jeans as he saw video after video of young, sexy college boys slowly peeling off their socks, revealing the tender, tasty foot flesh underneath. This was a very common occurrence for the young man, and even after years of dutifully nurturing this fetish, letting it grow in size and scope, it didn't get any less boring.

Now that Kevin felt completely engulfed by his horny, glorious insobriety, precum no doubt already bleeding through the fabric of his boxers, Kevin defaulted next to a favorite activity of his: writing out e-mails that never get sent. He opened up another draft in his Gmail account, his cock pulsating in approval. He had over 60 e-mails saved in his drafts folder, all with friends names filled out in the "To:" field: dirty, naughty fetish confessions filling the e-mails' body. All these names of would-be recipients was a mish-mash of unobtainable eye-candy: current friends, co-workers, friends from school, etc. They were never sent because, well, Kevin never once wanted to actually ruin any one of these friendships, much less humiliate himself for real. It was a lot of fun, still, to fantasize about what he couldn't have, and by writing out actual e-mails -- naughty, humiliatingly candid missives that were written entirely in the heat of the moment -- he truly was indulging his love of self-inflicted (but tightly controlled) humiliation, of living on the edge, of almost being dangerous. It was a small act of horny submission to his own fetish, but few things truly got him harder.

Thus, a new page was open, and it didn't take long for Kevin to immediately think about his best friend Eric's feet. Those goddamn sexy hipster feet. Incredible for a twenty-something, truly in their prime. His perfectly shaped toes, his tender soles, those lickably curved arches, Eric's constant desire to be either sandal-clad or barefoot any given moment -- it gave the devious Kevin oodles of inspiration. One slightly unusual thought had been encircling his head as of late that concerned Eric's feet: just how jealous he was of that boy's sandals, getting to constantly hug and be pressed against those sweaty size 10s day in and day out. Thus, taking another swig of brew, Kevin got to writing yet another cum-fueled confession, touching his own denim-bound hardon in between paragraphs just to make sure he was still in the moment. His e-mail was as follows:

If I had a genie, Eric, you know what one of my first wishes would be?

I would love nothing more than to be your sandals for a day.

It's a strange concept -- I know how it sounds -- but there is absolutely nothing that I want more. You know I have a foot fetish, but I frequently wonder if you know how bad it is. I pop footboners on a daily basis, and the thing is: I fucking love it. I am conscious of how my fetish works, but I love feeding it, of finding that new batch of tender foot flesh that I want to submit to, praying I can trace the curve of those arches with the tip of my cock time and time again. Surely you know that you've been an unwilling participant in it. After all, you're barefoot around someone with a cripplingly powerful male foot fetish -- at some point it has to click for you. In many ways I'm glad we don't talk about it, but at the same token, part of me wishes you'd take advantage of me one of these days, of propping your exposed feet right in my lap, ordering me to massage them while making unrealistic demands that I would have to submit to, utterly hopeless to say no as you have simply handed me the Holy Grail of Horniness and who am I to say no? I value you as a friend, and as such I'd never do anything to violate that, but oh, if I could. Oh the things I'd do ...

... starting with actually becoming your sandals. I'd love to be the ones you have now: a solid slab of leather that has begrudgingly accepted the imprints of your bared feet, your toes in particular leaving ghost versions of themselves on there. To have those feet imprinted on me, to exist with their shape, their smell, even their taste tattooed on my person -- I truly can't think of anything I'd be prouder of wearing: existing to be under you, existing for the purpose of holding and comforting your sexy soles and toes and doing absolutely nothing else aside from wishing you wearing me when you weren't.

I can imagine how a typical day would go: you'd be sleeping, breathing quietly, and I'd be laying there on your cold hardwood floors, eagerly anticipating the moment when you'd wake up. I'd be eying the foot of your bed with great interest, hoping to catch a peak of your toes sticking out, your arches exposed, vulnerable, tender and delicious. You'd stir, you'd rise, you'd be groggy and run your fingers through your tussled brown hair. I'd wait for that moment when you swing your legs around until both feet are together, inches off the ground. I'd replay what happens next over and over again in slow motion: your toes landing first on the floor, the toes adjusting to the surface, the rest of your sole slowly pouring onto the hardwood, the heels landing like an exclamation point to a very sexy sentence. I love those moments when your toes unconsciously twitch, curling ever so slightly, adjusting to the coldness of the ground. You weren't expecting the floor to be this chill, even in the summer, were you? It's OK. You'd stand up and start to walk by me, myself getting excited that I might be lucky enough to come in contact with your foot flesh at so early an hour: but you never, ever do. I know you too well by now: you'll go to your computer to check your e-mail or go to your kitchen to grab breakfast or even take a shower, washing all that delicious footsweat away.

Yet, since I absorb your sweet, tasty footsweat on a daily basis, I assure that you're doing a great disservice to the world. That salty, tangy footsweat needs to be preserved, collected, sold in large quantities, used as icing on cakes. I practically take a bath in it every day, and it makes me want to explode with pleasure. I tingle the second it comes into contact with me, sending lightning bolts of pleasure through me. I wish I had a refrigerator filled with nothing but water bottles of your chilled footsweat. I'd soak in a bathtub full of it if not just so I could soak it up, imbuing me with the world's first permanent erection. Yet I digress ...

You'd clothe yourself, you'd fritter about as you do most mornings, applying to a schedule albeit haphazardly. There are days, I am loathe to admit, where you toss on some year-old ankle socks and the same black-and-white tennis shoes you have been wearing for ... hell, I lost track of when you got them. Still, in tandem, those pieces of manufactured footwear do a great job of capturing your enchanting footmusk, but I would argue I capture the essence of your bare feet far, far better: your sweat takes some time before it actually begins leaving an impression in me, showing time and dedication. There's a true permanence to how we work together, and I enjoy being a part of that history. You might walk by again, and I'll monitor every aspect of that step: your foot extending out an angle, the heel casually hitting the floor, that sole filling out, your toes angling the foot upward for takeoff again: it's quite the incredible sight. You may not see it, but your pinky toe never actually makes contact with the ground, and for some reason I find that unbelievably hot.

Then, of course, comes my favorite moment of all: you decide to go out for the day, and you pick me as your traveling companion. You wear your t-shirt and jeans, and casually walk yourself over to me, your whole godlike presence standing before me. I tremble at the thought of those feet being inches away from me, of ultimately completing me. Then, one foot lifts up barely off the ground and heads towards the toehold. My day is already made. That sexy big toe leads the way, every other raw toe following suit, slightly splayed, anticipating the fact that they'll be gripping onto me soon. Then, they make contact: the toehold, long soaked in your glorious footsweat, is gripped by your toes once again, and the rest of the

the foot follows, aligning with its imprinted shadow in me once again. Made for each other, practically. The other foot follows, and we are one. Harmonious existence has been achieved.

As you lock up the door to your apartment and head outside into the hot summer air, my absolutely favorite part of the day begins: your feet begin warming me whole. I feel the warmth radiate all over: from heel to toes, those toes wiggling a bit with each boner-popping step. I go from the cold temperature of the morning hardwood to the same heat as your warmblooded feet. What an honor. What a privilege Those sweat-blackened footstains on me are only going to get that much darker, and I thrill at the thought of it.

You continue to go through the rest of the day wearing me, sweating all the more, wiggling your toes unconsciously while you think, each toepad tapping against me, teasing me, exciting me. I keep thinking that these toe-tappings are actually some sort of Morse code I have yet to decipher, but I haven't figured it out. I keep thinking, however, that if there are messages, they simply would be acknowledgments along the lines of "Yeah, these toes keep you up at night, don't they?" No one could ever argue with a statement like that.

After a whole day about the city, your warm feet strapped to my person, imprints deepening, embedding me with your smell, you walk home and a sprinkler with bad placement covers me with a light film of water, which makes each step you take a little more frictionless, your toes sliding across my surface, touching areas that to this point have yet to he honored by the touch of your sexy digits. Moments like this I cherish. I goddamn love having new parts of me exposed to the downright greatness that is your feet and toes.

You get home and we head to your apartment. Even with your shortened indoor steps, I still get to make that sexy slapping sound of myself hitting the bottom of your heel time and time again. I wonder if after all these years I've had the privilege of shaping the bottoms of your heels in even the slightest of ways. To be a part of the history of feet so intensely orgasmic as yours is nothing short of a true honor. Sandals don't get the privilege of picking their podiacal partners in crime, but I feel blessed to be smeared with your footstink on a daily basis.

You open the door to your apartment, and in the foyer, do the one thing I absolutely hate: you casually kick me off. And then there I am on the floor, your footwarmth gradually fading from me. It's the saddest part of the day, and unless there's the chance of a late-night food run of some sort, I know our interactions are done for the night.

Yet even as you sleep, I dream of serving your masterful feet again. I dream of your toenails accidentally scraping against my surface, of the fingerprint-like ridges of your toepads rubbing against me, deepening that imprint just a little more, of your footsweat baking into me for all eternity.

Until then I wait, your loyal servant in the wings. I exist solely for your soles. Tomorrow, thankfully, is another day when I can do what I do best, and get to touch your bare, bare feet ...

Kevin's beer was drained down to not even half-a-swig. He ran spell check on the e-mail once again, pleased with the eloquence he was able to accomplish even while drunk. He did feel like those sandals sometimes: existing simply to serve, worship, and honor those deliriously erotic feet. There were fewer fantasies as utterly delicious, devious, and boner-inducing than what he thought about Eric's soft, pink feet. Man, this was turning into one hell of a great night.

Suddenly, he heard a little e-mail beep in one of his other e-mail accounts. He Alt-Tab'd over to his e-mail program, only to see that a piece of spam had worked its way into another account. Not in need of pills that would guarantee to increase his manhood, Kevin flipped back over to his browser to look at his wonderful new piece of horny fantasy ... but saw something odd. A little browser pop-up that said "Your message has been sent." Then, in a flash of intense horror, Kevin suddenly remembered something about Gmail: Alt-

Enter is a hotkey for sending an e-mail. He knew he hit Alt-Tab, but if in his intoxicated state he completely forgot ...

Oh fuck.

The next day, Kevin's private fetish life was forever altered, and little did he know that his ultimate humiliation had only just begun ...

THE MARKET

+ + +

Here it is: my epic. My epic to end all epics. The biggest, most jam-packed, overstuffed story I have ever written. The basic idea, you'll notice, incorporates a lot of elements from my earlier stories, ranging from "The Chip" to "The Gallery", but here boosted by an arc and man's self-discovery that when faced with a ticklish torture that he hates more than anything else in the world, sometimes the only way out is through. It's the story of one of the nicest, sweetest guys you know running a life that is tragically ordinary, at least until this unexpected set of events -- all starting with him wearing flip-flops just one day to work -- leads him on an erotic journey where he must overcome exhaustion, intense humiliation, and the desires of others in order to make it through to the other side, coming out the end all the strong because of it. I loosely based this off of someone I know but wound up tossing in dozens of cameos from real-life friends of mine, a great majority of them who probably don't even know they're in here. This story took an awful long time to get off the ground, but once I started writing it, I couldn't stop, setting up every scene, every detail, and obsessing over the human element through it all, finding the emotion while layering scene upon scene of unbridled tickle torture and forced foot worship. I still can't believe I actually finished it, but what an absolutely joyous time I had writing it. Just keep this in mind next time you decide to show off some foot flesh at the office boy-o ...

Jon literally had no fucking clue.

There he was, walking around the office in the early Fall, wearing flip-flops, jeans, and a bright green zip-up vest. Right now, Jon felt pretty much how he always felt: like the *man*.

Of course, Jon wasn't a jerk or anything: in fact, he was one of the nicest guys in the whole office. Just a shade under six feet tall, in his late 20s, this former frat boy & occasional freestyle rapper (made all the more awkward by his obvious whiteness) had quite the checkered past, but he now had a stable girlfriend of three years, and was, to a degree, "settling into his routine" with life. Good workman-like teleconferencing job, good lady by his arm -- all things that actually turned out to be kind of boring for him, truth be told. He yearned for something greater, something more. Little did he know, however, that by wearing flip-flops today, he had started a chain of events that would take him into territories he never knew existed, forever altering the course of his life.

Jon could be seen as quiet in the eyes of some, but he still had his passions. He had a great love of pop music, a great aversion to all things related to politics, and a fairly good passion for shoes (he had literally dozens of pairs). He just liked having a great collection of shoes to chose from, ranging from fancy to tennis to casual to sandal. He could easily go through two weeks without wearing the same pair twice. Although he owned a set of sandals, he wore it so irregularly that their occasional appearance was definitely worth mentioning, particularly for one of his co-workers, Tommy.

Tommy was a bit of an eccentric (he wore a tie to work every day, even if it meant wearing it during the summers when it complimented his khaki shorts and flip-flops), but was still a nice guy, a hard worker, and owner of a deviously intense male foot and tickle fetish. As cool and calculated as Tommy was on the surface (and on the occasional blue moon, someone would call him "cool," often in some hipster-related context), he was almost completely helpless to his very specific fetishes. They absolutely dominated his sexual landscape, and they would be dangerously close to defining him had he not had enough social grace to mask what turned him on in casual conversation. His co-workers were easy targets, of course, because, well, when you spend 9-10 hours a day with the same people in and out, it's hard not to catch the occasional glance, share in the slightly inappropriate joke, and occasionally fumble towards the odd bit of erotic fantasy now and then.

Thus, Tommy always viewed Jon as a bit of an attractive guy. He never thought of Jon as someone he could have an emotional attachment to, but seeing the never-ending selection of shoes Jon paraded around in, Tommy's mind couldn't help but wander and wonder what the bare feet of such an extraordinary specimen must look like. Thus, catching a view of Jon's raw toes today in the office -- pale, nicely rounded, unquestionably sexy -- did something to Tommy's brain that has only happened once a decade it seems: it set his sexual fantasies absolutely on fire. Those pink toes coming out from under the bottom rims of dark blue jeans: they looked positively succulent, full of flavor, and popped an instant footboner in Tommy's pants. Even after five seconds of viewing them, it was all Tommy's eyes needed to have their image imprinted on his brain forever. Never one to be too jealous or selfish, the hornier parts of his personality came to an immediate confusion: it absolutely *had* to have those feet.

During his bus ride home from work, Tommy's subconscious immediately reimagined about 247 different scenarios wherein he could extract pleasure out of Jon's plump digits, almost all of them 100% impossible to actually do in reality. Thus, that night, Tommy did what any good fetishist would do: he got high and proceeded to jack off to those numerous erotic daydreams his brain concocted earlier. These included being dominated by Jon, having those smelly soles pushed directly into his face, to suck on Jon's toes while he slept, to tie him up naked and blindfolded while teasing and tickling every single exposed nerve ending he could find, driving him bonkers with forced horniness before making him explode -- you know, the usual. There was just one problem with properly articulating any of those fantasies into the real world: in this day and age, tickling was completely, totally illegal.

About five years prior, there was an LSU frat pledge named Patrick Lund who wanted to really get into Tao Kappa Lambda (his Frat of choice), but he had to go through a pledge Hell Week that was unlike anything he had ever experienced: he was tied up and mercilessly tickled by his fellow brothers for eight consecutive hours. The bros who lorded over him spent all night drinking, smoking, and intoxicating themselves before taking turns seeing who could get the highest octaves out of the bound, screaming bit of tickleflesh known as Patrick. In truth, after the second hour of torture, Patrick's body had pretty much shut down wholesale, refusing to even put up a fight. Fingernails scratched the soft, helpless center of his bare soles, feathers danced across his nipples and twirled around his quivering stomach, and five-finger attacks were carried out on his armpits, ribcage, and underarms. Patrick screamed for the first two hours, whined for the third, and spent the other five, desperate, crying, begging and whimpering. The guys were never cruel or forceful but so much tickling at one time left bruises on Patrick's skin, especially in the ribcage area. Once they finally released the boy, he immediately, unconsciously curled into the fetal position and passed out, eventually sleeping for 18 uninterrupted hours. When he awoke back at his dorm room (his brothers must've transported him back in his slumber), his limbs ached in pain, having spent a third of an entire day flexing, straining, and struggling.

Unlike the other pledges who were immediately invited into the fraternal brotherhood following this ordeal (as they had done for years), Patrick filed suit against the frat and the university. Instead of lying down and taking it, the fight grew bitter, slowly gaining statewide attention before capturing a national audience. Appeals begat appeals, and when the Supreme Court weighed in, in a shocking move, not only did they side with young Patrick (who received a hefty amount of damages), they also labeled tickling as an abusive act. Following the decision, some acts of seemingly-innocent tickling could be construed as abusive, leading to arrests or even lawsuits. In fact, the number of lawsuits that followed in the SCOTUS ruling (which quickly became known as "the Lund Decision", an association which ironically would follow Lund his entire life, constantly the bunt of tickle-related jokes and cat calls, which is now perhaps why no one has heard from him in over a year) were surprising in sheer quantity. Against all possible odds, tickling, for all intensive purposes, was made illegal. Liberal causes cited this as the government intruding into people's bedrooms, but it'd be years before a proper challenge to the Lund Decision would be heard. Couples at home had to be discreet about their bedroom activities, for fear of arrest or even a lawsuit. It was, in short, a bizarre, terrifying time to live.

All of this, however, didn't stop those with true tickle fetishes. People met in discreet clubs to indulge their fantasies, and -- perhaps most surprisingly -- Tommy found that there was a nefarious rumor around the internet about a black market for tickle slaves: all involving young men who were kidnapped and sold off to the highest bidder for the sole purpose of being nothing more than ticklish pleasure toys to their new masters. While this all seemed like the basis for a forum goon to spread salacious rumors or a fanfic story being horribly misconstrued as truth, Tommy Googled, forum searched, and did every possible thing he could to find out more about if this was real or not. His brain's melding with his fetish was far too permanent: he *had* to know if this was real or not, and would not rest until he discovered the dirty truth.

Yet the truth of the matter was that Tommy was very conflicted. You see, he very much liked Jon. He liked Jon a lot, in fact. They occasionally grabbed lunch together at work, they shared jokes and stupid YouTube videos, and were even each others Secret Santa at work by fate of fates. Tommy would even go as far to say that they were friends, and as much as Tommy had a laundry list of fantasies he want to unleash on Jon, he could never bring himself to do anything about it: the friendship was far more important.

That being said, Tommy did have his dark moments: those days when he was high as a kite, horny from not having jacked off for days on end, and in those moments of pure erotic weakness, his desires took over, resulting him taping incriminating confessions or making videos of him jacking off to candid foot photos he had taken of his friends and co-workers. During one of these nights, he was in his apartment alone, stoned, whacking away at his curved, beet-red cock, pulsating with fetishy pleasure as he ogled the completely candid photos he took of Jon's exposed, sandaled toes. Before climaxing though (which was more of an inevitability than ever before), he opened up a bookmark he had of a web forum he stumbled upon that, against all odds, was not listed on any search engine. It was for what appeared to be an organization called the Black Feather, which claimed to be one of those mysterious "black market" syndicates hell-bent on rounding up the oh-so-ticklish and forcing them to live out the rest of their lives as helpless sexual playthings. Their website was nothing more than a simple form that asked three things: the "Potential's" name, place they could be found, and why they'd be good for the Black Feather to procure (the only writing below the submission areas said "Serious inquiries only."). Stoned, horny, and clearly not thinking straight, Tommy proceeded to fill out the form as follows:

NAME: Jon Smith.
PLACE: The 7th floor of 800 Adams Ave, Philadelphia
WHY: Oh god. Man. So many reaszins. He wore sandals for the first time ever last week. He NEVERR wears sandals. Like ever. He has a differnt pair of shoes he wears every day. Guy oviousl y takes good care of his feet, and those soles must be soft as fuck. He's a nice guy, but god there is no way he's not ticklishh as hell. He might even be the most ticklish boy in the world. He once tokd a story about how he had to stop a pedicure at one point not only cos he doesn't like peoplpe near his feet but that his feet were reacting ticklish to every single touch and he couldn't take it. Would love nothing more than to have a shot at him.

Tommy didn't even proofread his submission: he just hit the big red SUBMIT button on the site, brought up the folder of Jon's toe pics he had on his computer, and had a remarkably satisfying climax, gobs of thick cum lapping out of him in waves, ruining his current shirt until laundry day. Soon thereafter, he cleaned himself up and passed out in a blissful slumber, a satisfied, glowing smile hanging off the corner of his face.

The following morning, Tommy awoke, hit snooze on his alarm, and accepted the fact that yes, it was Monday. He slowly got out of bed, had a bowl of cereal, a quick wank in the shower, and made it to work. Just before groggily reaching his cubicle, he passed by Jon's cubical, gave him a quick "hey", and took note of Jon's shoe choice today: red Chuck Taylors. Not bad. The conversation ended, Tommy walked away, and retained that glorious image of Jon's shoes in his mind. Would be all Tommy would get to help him through a long, boring Monday.

Sometime after lunch when Tommy was blankly staring at his computer, he suddenly remembered something: last night, he stupidly submitted some information about Jon on a shady website, and he totally had to remove it. Discreetly looking around to make sure his co-workers weren't looking, he tried to type in what he thought was the Black Feather's web address a few times (recalling from memory was hard, and stumbled upon more than one fan site about the movie *Black Swan*). Eventually he found it, that same simple, unadorned submission page as before. He hovered his mouse over every pixel for a link to anything else he could find, but to no avail. Being a bit of an amateur HTML coder, he tried looking up the webpage's source code to get hints about who to talk to or where his information about Jon went. The code, tragically, was very simple, the info having gone to a remarkably secure Google spreadsheet. Tommy's level of panic was increasing more and more: what if this was real?

Tommy rushed home from work as fast as he could, jumping immediately on his personal computer to look up the Forums where he initially heard about the Black Feather. He asked questions about how to get in touch with them, if anyone knew if any *actual* kidnapping had taken place, etc. He got a lot of "idk" responses, a couple crazy rambles -- nothing of substance to speak of. Tommy's panic increased more and more, but after a few soothing glasses of Scotch, his worries subsided: c'mon, who *really* would do this? This is just wackiness. Like any organization would have the funding and the gall to kidnap young men to be tickle torture victims on user-submitted whims like that. That's just stupid. Comforting himself, Tommy's brain allowed itself to feel relaxed about the situation. The nervous tension wasn't completely gone, but it had noticeably subsided, and Tommy was able to actually get to sleep at a halfway decent hour.

The next day, Tommy began working his way to his cubicle, and passed Jon's along the way. However, Jon wasn't there. He hunted down Jon's manager Don, a burly bear of a man who still was only his late 20s, obviously some sort of ex-football player in college. Tommy inquired as to where Jon was (making up some bullshit story about how he was working with Jon on a weird report he was dealing with), and Don said that Jon had called in sick for the day. It was odd, for sure, as Jon almost never took sick days, but it is what it is. As he walked back to his desk, Tommy's more paranoid thoughts took hold and began running through scenarios about what was going on, all culminating in the surprising, sudden abduction of Jon by the Black Feather. Again, Tommy calmed his thoughts, assuring himself that everything was normal, and his brain was just going a bit on the crazy end of things.

The following day, Tommy walked by Jon's cubicle -- still not there. In fact, by the time Friday rolled around, Tommy noticed that Jon hadn't come in at all. He went to Don one more time that Friday, and Don -- starting to get annoyed with Tommy's multitude of inquiries -- said that it appeared Jon had applied for an elongated medical leave, the condition causing this something that he couldn't disclose to a fellow employee. When Tommy asked if Jon would ever be back, Don replied "Hard to say. From the sounds of it, he could be gone for good -- which is fine, 'cos his health is far more important than any job he could be doing." Tommy thanked Don before trying to leave, Don stopping him in the doorway saying that Tommy should forward up the project he was "urgently" working on with Jon so he could take it over. While being caught in a lie like this was no doubt one of the most unpleasant feelings one could go through, the more paranoid parts of Tommy's brain couldn't contain themselves. Something just didn't feel right. Something was definitely "off." This was not good.

When Tommy got home from work that day, he checked the mailbox of his apartment complex, and saw that he had received ...

a very odd note. A jet-black high-gloss envelope that simply said "You are invited ..." on the front of it. When Tommy opened it up, his eyes went wide with terror ...

+ + +

Jon got home from another hectic day of work. There are times where he became disillusioned with his job, but sometimes coming home to a girl like Sandra made all the difference. She was a go-getting girl who was an account manager for a global telecommunications company, so her job was a bit more hectic than Jon's: often, she'd simply doze off to whatever movie or TV show they wound up watching (usually *Game of Thrones* -- Sandra didn't understand half of what was going on with that show). Tonight, however, was different. As Jon was in their bedroom slowly removing his fancy new two-week old shoes (nice brown leather finish, zippers along the outside ankles), Sandra seemed to be gallivanting about, fretting over something on her laptop. Often she was disinterested when checking her work email from home, but tonight was different. Something was happening. As Jon walked sockfooted down their duplex's staircase to the kitchen, Sandra appeared to be getting ready to leave again.

"Hey hon," started Jon, "what, um, seems to be going on?"

"God, I don't even know," she started in her familiar stressed-but-working-on-it voice. "Something started up at the office just as I left work. Some say it's a virus attack or a decimal point horridly out of place, but the numbers on all our accounts seem to be out of whack and our backups haven't kicked in. I think I gotta go in and babysit this until it's over."

"But hon, that's not really your department area."

She laughed a bit. "I know, but I got the hard copies and need to verify everything. You gon' be OK fending for food by your lonesome?"

"We have a microwave, don't we?"

They kissed as she grabbed her car keys. "See you whenever I get back darling," she said. "Right back atcha," said Jon, only marginally sad that he had the place to himself.

Two hours later, he was laying his bed, DVR catching up on the latest *Game of Thrones* while his fingers dived into the remnants of a bowl of KFC chicken that he picked up only an hour before. Bachelor night to the nth degree. The volume was turned up, but Jon suddenly felt that he heard something. Disconcerted, he hit pause on his remote and listened for a moment. Nothing. Just the air from the vent and nothing more. He hit play again and turned the volume up even louder than before, wanting very much to get transported to another world, one with beheading and dwarves and a surprising about of on-screen nudity. The show played on for about three more minutes and then, in a flash, the entire duplex went dark. "Dammit," Jon thought, convinced a fuse had gone out once again. He wiped his chicken-greased hands on his jeans (of course), swung his legs over to the side of the bed and started his way to the downstairs fusebox. The second he opened his bedroom door, however, a litany of black gloved hands filled his vision near instantaneously. Jon would've reacted had it not been so quick, but his mouth was covered, his eyes blinded, and his arms restrained in what seemed like nanoseconds. Before he could even form an alarmed thought, Jon tasted something funny in his mouth, and before hew knew it, was unconscious.

+++

Jon's eyes struggled to open, his head feeling like it was in the middle of a terrible cold, all stuffy and wildly unfocused. Groggy was the best term he could use. As his eyelids raised, a lot of white light was pouring into his vision, and it took a moment to adjust. He tried to move his arm to rub his eyes ... but he couldn't. What was going on? Was he paralyzed? Where was he? He then noticed that ... he was in mid-air -- and he was naked. His arms were directly above him, restrained in some sort of oddly futuristic-looking mechanical contraption. His legs were behind him, held in similar, leaving Jon's body somewhat at an angle, his stomach facing the floor, all at a 45 degree angle or so, his bare feet closer to the floor than his head. Jon started panicking, immediately struggling within his bonds, but he couldn't budge an inch: the padding for the restraints on his arms and ankles was comfortable but solid -- he couldn't move a half-inch. His legs were spread apart only a bit (the same width as regular standing position, Jon determined), but it meant his junk was simply out there, flapping in the breeze. It was humiliating to say the least.

His panic was palpable but controlled; his brain slowly began turning that panic into a series of "what do I do now?" kind of thoughts. His eyes scanned the the room looking for anything that would help him. To his surprise, it was surprisingly barren: light gray concrete lining up the walls, solid-white fluorescent lights overhead, a lit-from-beneath white plastic floor below. The whole thing had a very clinical look to it, although the air temperature was surprisingly warm all things considered. If Jon had to make a guess, he'd guess that wherever he was it was somewhere underground, the whole thing seeming like it was once used as a lair for a James Bond villain. His eyes scanned for tables filled with disemboweling tools, lasers to cut him open from the ceiling, anything that could hurt him (or help him) -- and there was nothing; just a door at the end of the room facing him and that was it (with the way he was restrained, he couldn't get a good view of the wall behind him, but he was pretty sure there wasn't a door from what he could gather).

While Jon's body tensed and contracted even at the thought of what kind of predicament he was in, his body somewhat relaxed after a whole 10 minutes passed and nothing happened. In fact, 10 more minutes passed and Jon began wondering if, somehow, he had been forgotten. Then, faintly, he could hear the very faint, muffled sound of footsteps coming from what the other side of the door opposite him. Suddenly, the glass wall slid open, and Jon saw a man walking towards him: white dress shoes, black-and-purple vertical striped three-piece suit, and a yellow/orange handkerchief tied around his neck. The man had a slight bit of a mustache, black hair slicked back, appearing to be in his early/mid-30s. The man took a very casual stroll towards the helpless, naked, confused and scared ex-frat boy.

"Hello Jon. My name is Gustav," the man said calmly.

"Dude, you gotta let me out. I don't know what's going on," Jon immediately blurted out without even thinking.

"Oh Jon, that is adorable. Trust me: you got a lot to learn," started Gustav, who began slowly walking around the suspended boy with a very deliberate stride. "First off, you can get rid of any notions that you're in a bad dream or having a psychedelic flashback of any sort. Yes, this is all very, very real, and you are very, very captured. You know by now that your restraints are on very tight, and you aren't going anywhere for a very, very long while."

"What?" screamed Jon, suddenly struggling again almost subconsciously, "Why the fuck would you do this to me? The fuck did I do?"

"Really Jon? Foul language? From you?" uttered Gustav, disappointed. "In all your college years you rarely swore. Not to your frat brothers, not to Sandra, not to anyone."

Jon's face turned surprised, frightened. "How do you know that?"

"Oh Jon, we vet every single submission we receive here. We are nothing but thorough. We only want grade-A stock and absolutely nothing less. We looked into your background, into your family, into your friends, into your work, into what you do in the bedroom and how frequently you do it. We have psychological profiles, we have bank statements, we have everything. In fact, you might as well forget your bank numbers altogether, as they are ours now."

"Who are you?" Jon asked, fearing menace.

Gustav continued his previous train of thought without stopping. "We're submitting various forms to get you out of work, we're crafting an elaborate backstory to make your loved ones think you are away on business -- sneak preview: you'll die from a foreign virus while being away -- and any assets that might be of interest to your bidders have already been collected. While it's not my thing necessarily, your worn leather sandals seemed to have generated a lot of interest amidst those parties that fancy that kind of thing. Well done."

Jon dismissed that seeming compliment that was just hurled at him. "What the fuck are you talking about? Tests? Collecting my stuff? 'Bidders'? The hell you going to do to me?"

"Oh," started Gustav, pleasure dripping from each word, "we're going to be doing a lot to you. I'm lucky enough to be assigned to you for your demonstration. For now, however, I have to do one last test before we go forward."

A mechanical sound could be heard from the ceiling above Jon. Whirring gears and sounds. Jon kept his focus on Gustav though.

"What are you talking about?" asked Jon.

Before Gustav could respond, a black hood was drawn over Jon's head very tightly. Jon immediately struggled, but it fit on him very quickly and very snugly. He couldn't see, he could barely make words, but could oddly breathe just fine. Unseen below him, Gustav walked up and placed two small plastic devices on each of Jon's nipples. They stayed on like suction cups, and Jon immediately began thrashing about, wondering what the hell was going to happen to him next. A minute had passed while Jon struggled an screamed as much as he could through his tight hood, but nothing happened. His body, still tense, simply sagged a bit in its restraints, awaiting something horrible. Instead, Jon heard a faint electronic click, and suddenly he felt something on each of his nipples. It was ... almost ... like a tongue? He knew they couldn't be human tongues (he was just far enough off the ground to prevent someone from doing that), but it felt moist, very flesh-like, very ... pleasurable. These two swirling tongues were lapping the area around his nips, dragging slowly over every sensitive nipplebud, slowly getting a rise out of the nipples wholesale. His protruding nip-tips were moved around by the simulated tongues, teased and pushed, lapped at and played with. Jon was ... enjoying this?

Gustav noticed it as soon as Jon felt it: a bit of a twitch in Jon's dangling cock. It was still just hanging from the suspension, but there was a little movement now in his limp meat stick. The nipples lapped and lapped and lapped and slowly, surely, that cock was becoming engorged with blood. Lap lap lap. It was at half-mast. Then, Jon suddenly felt a hand (presumably Gustav's) reach out and give his member a little tug -- that woke it up and brought it to attention. A few more tugs -- brief, but forceful, and suddenly Jon was in mid-air, blindfolded, getting his nipples licked by machines and harboring a surprising erection given his plight. Jon's cock was solidly long and cleanly circumcised, his cockhead sprouting a very nice, textured rim. Gustav thought it was actually quite beautiful.

Yet with no time for niceties, Gustav reached into his jacket and pulled a small, black device. There were small black bars all over it, as it was meant to latch onto erect cocks such as Jon's. Quickly, he snapped the device into place, one metal ring at the thick base of Jon's member and another right underneath the rim of his cockhead. There was a retractable metal arm connecting the two rings and a light motor at the ring near his base. Gustav flicked a switch on the motor, and away it went: the two rings drew close together, then spread apart, then came together again, then spread apart and so forth. The device began jacking the boy against his will, and the feeling was causing an immediate adrenaline rush through Jon's body. Pump. Stop. Pummmmp. Stop. The machine was varying its speeds, so Jon couldn't adjust or get into any sort of "groove" whatsoever. Instead, the mechanical tongues kept him horny by his nipples while his cock was slowly being driven to the point of orgasm and back. Pummmp. It went. Jon tried as he couldn't, but he was beginning to realize that he couldn't control his horniness anymore: the devices were controlling it for him. Jon was getting sexually frustrated to the nth degree -- he's never had control of his own orgasm wrenched away from him so blatantly like this before -- but the machines were guiding his body closer and closer to an extreme orgasm, even as his mind wanted to hold off and "enjoy it" more.

Pump. Stop. Pummmmmmmmmpump. Stop. Jon's fevered brain could barely take it anymore. He felt those tingles of pleasure collection at the tip of his cockhead, driving him insane. All Jon could think about was how badly he wanted to cum, how badly he wanted to shoot out rockets of white hot cum, feeling wave upon wave of pleasure, tingles reaching every single crevice of his body, oh god he was almost at the edge. *Fuck, just let me cum already!*

Gustav's fingers teased the undersides of Jon's balls briefly, feather touches that circled. That sent Jon over the edge.

Jon's cock gave one last pump before firing out a rocket of his white-hot seed, Jon almost screaming through his hood while it did so. The erotic lightning he felt dissipated all over his crotch, the machine attached continuing to pump at uneven rates without stopping because it was just a machine, incapable of mercy. Another shot fired out of the boy, and then another, and then Jon's cock was beginning to feel too sensitive. The pumps continued, and Jon was starting to become all too aware of how sensitive his blood-red manhood was getting. "Please stop," he said into the muffled hood, little drops of cum continuing to ooze out of his head against his will. "Please stop!" he shouted, again muffled. Yet the pumps continued, and they almost kind of hurt but not really just because he was so damn sensitive. Jon thought he couldn't take another one, but it continued to pump, those rings sliding up and down his shaft, and Jon screamed as loud as he could into the hood, unable to take anymore, his body shuddering as he did so.

Gustav flicked the switch off the device, and Jon's body practically went limp. Gustav could see a great deal of sweat had accumulated in Jon's pits, and the boy's chest began heaving desperately, taking in giant hits of air to try and replenish even a little of the strength that he had prior. Gustav walked around, seemingly pleased with the results. Jon could hear the faint muffled sound of whirring mechanical parts, and suddenly some robotic arms removed the tight hood from his head with extreme ease. Sweat had made his hair damp, and it was slathered across his forehead in a messy fashion (Gustav would go as far as to call the look sexy). Jon just sagged there, impossibly tired from his sudden sexual ordeal. Gustav smirked.

"You know," Gustav started, "as unexpected as that was, that actually wasn't the test itself, sweet Jon." Gustav was now positioned behind the suspended Jon, standing in-between his legs, eyes facing Jon's back. "Everything you just experienced was prep. Glorious prep. Because the real test -- the real reason why you're here -- begins right now ..."

And with that, Gustav dug his middle and index fingers into the sides of Jon's belly.

Jon yelped in falsetto.

That yelp quickly dissolved into hysterical laughter, however, as Gustav's fingers prodded and wiggled around in Jon's sides, and Jon -- a man who hated being tickled since as far back as he could remember -- immediately struggled harder than he ever had his life. His body swayed side to side and up and down as much as it could, but it couldn't escape Gustav's expert finger-work: one hand circled while the other prodded, and then they switched, and then one zig-zagged fingernails across the underside of Jon's belly, and index finger writhed around inside Jon's belly button, and the torture was 100% non-stop. Jon felt his shoulder spasm, his foot twitch, and all manner of his muscles freaking out in unexpected ways. Gustav was now kneeling on the ground underneath Jon, fingers spidering into Jon's sensitive ribcage, playing the boy like an accordion, squeezing every last possible note of laughter he could out of him. Jon's mouth was stretched so far into a smile it hurt, and the worst part was that Jon didn't even want to smile: he hated being tickled more than just about anything else he could imagine and here he was, helpless, taking it. Sweat dripped out of him like a wet sponge being twisted. It was insanity.

Gustav, however, was loving it. "You're a remarkable specimen," he noted to the laughing boy. "I don't think you're going to have any problem finding a home." By this time, Gustav was now facing

Jon, and by stretching his arms up high, Gustav's fingers could easily work their way into Jon's armpits, and the second that index finger poked that soft patch of light pitflesh (wiggling around inside shortly thereafter), Jon lost it, unable to fight anymore, his body bucking and braying, his mouth a direct line of communication to the gods of laughter, his own voice and words completely unable to get through. Wiggle wiggle wiggle went Gustav's fingers, squeezing every last drop of laughter they could out of the boy, Gustav grinning having finally found Jon's "spot". All Jon's brain was filled with was tickling, tickles, how much this tickles, please don't tickle me there, dear god no, why my armpits, tickle tickle tickle, fuck no, more tickles, tickle.

Without warning, Gustav stopped tickling Jon altogether, Gustav's hands covered in pitsweat which he wiped off on a kerchief just as Jon's continued to laugh, the aftershocks continuing on for over a minute without halting. Finally, the laughs whimpered out of him less and less, and Jon's head fell forward, his eyes sagging downward, and before long, the boy had passed out. Gustav grinned again, knowing his work was done. He slowly began to walk out of the room, knowing full well that Jon's next 24 hours were going to be a whirlwind.

+ + +

Jon awoke, groggy. As the light of the room began slowly filling in, Jon's body immediately tried to move again and -- nothing. He was in the same position as he was before. Yet as his mind slowly began waking up, Jon noticed that something was different: he was in a different room than he was before. Although he was suspended in the exact same way, Jon noticed that his arms didn't feel tired, nor did his stomach feel empty. Although he couldn't know for sure, his only guess as to what happened was that between seeing Gustav and now, he was let out and ... fed? He had no memory of any of that, but there is no reason why his body should feel as comfortable as it should right now.

Jon's eyes looked around: he was in glass box -- no wider than 6'x6' -- housed in a much larger room with similar aesthetics to the last. He looked over to his right and saw ... another person. Another guy, suspended. As Jon's vision adjusted, he could see that in this room, there were actually all sorts of guys in glass cubes, restrained from the ceiling in the exact same fashion that he was. Together, there was one door to this room (and it was a big one), and Jon and his fellow captives formed a U around the door, almost as if they were at some sort of exhibit. Jon could even see someone suspended immediately across from him, facing him. The guy across from him still hadn't woken up, but was a much more portly fellow, still suspended all the same. To his left was a young, scruffy young guy with black, messy hair, an almost-beard, and visible-but-not-overpowering hair on his arms and legs. To his right was a muscled, high school football captain-type, shoulders broad, blond hair with a buzzcut. He was awake and clearly panicking, hyperventilating as he looked around to see all the other guys around him in the exact same predicament (Jon estimated that there were about a dozen or so in the room). The jock and Jon made eye contact. The jock said something but Jon couldn't hear a word -- their glass pens must be soundproof. Jon stared more intently and could see the jock mouthing out the words "help me" with a panicked look on his face. Jon, more calm than his comrade, gestured to his restraints with his eyes, as if saying "What the hell could I possibly do?" Jon then noticed something odd on the guy's cell directly across from him: at the very base of his glass cage, there was a large video monitor on the floor that tilted up and out a bit, as if it was going to show a video to someone observing the suspended boy face-to-face. In fact, there was a monitor like this in front of every single cage. Something was going on, but Jon couldn't tell what.

Suddenly, classical music came booming through everyone's cell, causing every single one of the captured men to look up as to where it's coming from. It sounded familiar, regal. Bach, maybe? Before his brain could process the orchestral work, the large door in the room opened up slowly, and there were literally dozens of well-dressed men that began slowly walking towards the U of helpless men. Jon noticed that every single video monitor flipped on for every cell, and every single one was showing a different video. Jon squinted and could see that, in fact, each monitor seemed to be playing a video of each respective victim being ... tickled? Jon couldn't make out the details but he could tell that in the video of the larger guy across from him, that poor soul wasn't being worked over by Gustav -- he was being worked over by two guys who were clearly having a ball on that man's helpless flesh.

Jon began observing the numerous clothed people slowly moving through the space, observing each cell and victim like they were a Rembrandt or Picasso. The men observing were of all sorts and types: a few dressed up in tuxedos, a few were wearing T-shirts and jeans, a few with blazers over their ironic indie-rock T-shirts. Quite a few of them had beers in hand, a few had glasses of champagne, but all of them reeked of money. Some were much older, but the mean age seemed to be around early 30s from what Jon could tell. A few started gathering in front of his cell, observing the monitors, a few guffaws and group chuckles emerging from the men looking at these videos. A few had already started to gather around Jon's cell, and he could see their faces alternate between staring at the video and then reaching back up towards Jon's face. Jon grimaced a bit when he made eye contact with a complete stranger, but none of them seemed to mind. As the numerous men gathered around the various cells, Jon managed to spot Gustav in the crowd, walking casually, paying no particular mind to any of the victims. From a distance, he looked directly at Jon and they made eye contact -- Gustav just winked at him. Jon was again very unnerved.

Soon, Jon noticed that every once in awhile, someone would come up to Gustav and ask a question. They would smile and then Gustav would pull out a small digital device of some sort. Gustav and the man who was approaching him presently walked over to the cell of the jock immediately to Jon's right. Gustav pressed a button his device and suddenly the entire back panel of the jock's cell slid open. Again, Jon couldn't hear anything over the classical music, but could see the jock desperately try to look behind him as he was slowly being lowered closer to the ground. The man who asked Gustav to see him walked right up to the boy's downward-pointing feet (which were now about waist level for the man) and he began to drag his fingernails across the jock's soles. Jon could see the jock screaming, shivering, struggling, but the man continued tickling away, driving the muscled football captain up the wall with hysteria. It wasn't even a minute before Jon could see tears starting to fall down from the jock's eyes. The man stopped his devious act and turned to Gustav, a smile on his face. Both walked back to the center of the U and Gustav pressed another button on his device, and before long the jock was elevated back to his previous suspended height while the glass door closed behind him. Gustav proceeded to unlock the cells for various men over and over again, each time seeing a guy get tickled by hand against his will, more often than not right on his bare feet. It's almost like each person was "testing" the victim in question.

Jon's eyes went back to the front of his own cell, and he could see that there was actually quite a substantial crowd gathered in front of him. A lot of people seemed to really like what they saw on the video. A lot of people were approaching Gustav, but he seemed to be dismissive of the people that approached him from Jon's crowd, like he didn't want to let anyone else handle Jon. Really, Jon did not know what to think of that gesture.

Suddenly, there was a bit of a commotion in the crowd as it was clear someone was moving to the front. Jon suddenly saw -- some kid. Some 20-something kid who made his way to the front of his cell, and the crowd was giving him a wide berth. It was clear that this kid was *somebody*, although he didn't look it: dark blue jeans, a dark blue blazer over a bright red T-shirt, white-rimmed sunglasses wrapped around his face. There was a taller, bald man standing directly behind this kid, dressed like a secret service member of some sort. Jon figured that that guy was to protect him. Apparently this kid was important, and right now the important kid wearing the sunglasses indoors was positively transfixed by Jon's video. He didn't bother to look up for several minutes, but as soon as he did, the kid smiled and gestured over to Gustav. He said something to him that caused the rest of the crowd to go up all up in arms, but Gustav seemed to manage the situation well, calming people down, making frequent gestures to the kid. Occasionally an arm went up, Gustav began saying something, then someone else's arm went up. Was ... was there an auction going on? Were people bidding on Jon? It didn't seem to matter: the kid countered every hand raise with one of his own, smiling, obviously intent to win whatever this was. By the end, Gustav pointed to the kid who threw up his arms in victory. The kid then turned and looked at Jon again, smiling in a positively devious fashion. He then walked over to Gustav and the two made their way behind Jon's glass cage, and Jon could hear the door open while he was slowly lowered. The second the door opened, Jon could hear the sounds of numerous conversations flooding in -- these doors really were sound-proof! It sounded like a party was going on. While Jon again couldn't really look behind him to see what's going on, he could clearly make out Gustav's voice.

"... indeed, I think this might be one of my favorites."

"Well," started what Jon assumed was the kid, "that video was impressive. Didn't fight you too hard either?"

"No," said Gustav, "seems like he could either be a really great submissive or could be playing a very smart game. My money? Submissive."

"I'm right here, ya know," said Jon out loud. It appears the men ignored him.

"Still, to set a record like that sir, it's very ..."

"Pfft, if the product's good, it's worth paying for," said the kid.

"In fact, sir, would you like --"

"Hi there," started a voice that Jon was unfamiliar with.

"Ah yes," started Gustav, "this is the young man who found this particular specimen."

"Well," started the kid, "thank you so much. I can tell you already that I'm going to have a lot of fun with this. You should keep up your hunting skills, fella -- this is top-notch pick right here."

"Well," started the unfamiliar voice, "is this the last time I'll get to see him?"

"Yes," said Gustav, flatly.

"Um, well," the voice continued, "do you mind if I ... I did one thing to him I've been absolutely dying to do for years?"

The kid laughed. "Heh, of course. I know how it is, and by all means."

Suddenly, Jon felt a pair of hands softly grab his right foot, slowly caressing and feeling it, tracing the vein lines on the top of his feet before fondling with the toes.

"Wow," the mysterious voice said, "they feel like a dream."

"Well go ahead and give 'em a test drive," the kid said, "will be the only chance you'll get to indulge in this.

Suddenly, Jon grimaced as he felt a moist, wet tongue slap itself right onto the base of his right toes and slowly -- so slowly -- drag itself across his sole and up to his heel. As it dragged, Jon laughed, as fuck did it tickle. The tongue then did it again, and before long he heard the kid say "Oh hell, let me try," and then a separate tongue began lapping his left sole, although at a much faster pace. Soon those hungry mouths wrapped themselves around Jon's plump toes and began to really suck. Jon's toes pointed and curled in quick motion, as they tried to get away, saliva dripping its way right in-between his toes, tickling him in such an oddly intimate area. Jon was giggling, laughing, and jerking his body back and forth to try and escape his fate but it was to no use: his feet were treats for these men, and there's nothing he could do about it. Even with the laughter running through him, Jon still felt absolutely humiliated, completely naked in front of these clothed men while his toes were suddenly being treated liked Ring Pops. It was degrading to the nth degree.

The mouths stopped their sucking.

"Thank you," the mysterious voice said.

"No, thank *you*," said the kid. "Depending on how things go, this could be my finest addition yet to my collection."

"That's wonderful to hear, gentlemen," interjected Gustav, "but now that he's been procured, it's time to get our specimen ready, as I have several other sales to tend to."

"Gotcha," said the kid. "Alright, might as well say your goodbyes to him."

With that, the glass door shut and Jon was being lifted back to his previous height by his restraints. The crowd in front of his cage had dissipated and seemed to be focused on other specimens now, but a single figure worked its way to the front of his cage, glad in a single white T-shirt, some shorts, and ... a tie? Jon's face turned to horror when he saw Tommy standing in front of him, looking sheepish and embarrassed. Tommy looked right into Jon's face, and mouthed out a very remorseful "I'm sorry." Jon was shocked and horrified ... but so confused. Why would Tommy do this to him? Tommy had to be the one who was licking his feet just now. Was he ... was Tommy in total lust with Jon's feet? Was --

Jon suddenly heard the sound of fumes, and looked around: his box was filling up with some sort of invisible gas. Jon accidentally took a breath and suddenly felt ... tired. Shit, he was being knocked out, wasn't he? He felt more tired by the second, but his last view was fixated on Tommy, and before he went unconscious, mouthed out the word "Why?" to his former co-worker. With that, Jon passed out, failing to see a clearly-conflicted Tommy hang his head in shame moments afterward.

+ + +

Jon awoke, once again, groggy as hell (truth be told, this whole "waking up restrained in a new place" thing would be comical if it weren't so terrifying). He immediately took stock of his surroundings and position: he was in a different room than he was before, and, fuck, again he was restrained. Yet there was something different about this time though: for one, the room was very different. It was a very small room, somewhat smaller than the glass cage he was in previously. Yet this time out, ahead of him was a glass door that lead out to ... something he couldn't make out. The floor, walls, and ceiling were white, save for a single gray panel with buttons near the glass door. With his knees actually planted on the ground for once, Jon could look behind himself a bit easier, and did so that he could see what appeared to be a plain white wall. In looking behind him, he also noticed he was restrained very differently this time out: each ankle was restrained with chains, and each chain lead to a small hole in the respective floor corners of the wall behind him, meaning his legs were very, very spread out. However, he could still bend and move a bit because Jon's wrists were fasted together in some sort of metal contraption, which he saw was attached to a chain that lead up to the ceiling. What was different from other times was that this chain was very loose. Even with his legs spread apart, Jon could still rise to a kneeling position or even crawl around using his elbows. His mobility was very limited, but he had mobility none the less. In many ways, this was a blessing, a welcome change of pace from before, even if he still hated what was going on.

Jon could tell what was going to happen: as soon as they start dragging that chain up to the ceiling, his body would be lifted up and pulled taught, suspended in a reverse-Y position, leaving his armpits extremely vulnerable. For now, however, he could move around a bit, and while he enjoyed this undoubtedly-temporary range of motion, his mind kept racing back to the U-shaped gallery and Tommy. What the hell was his co-worker doing at this bizarre event, much less wanting to lick the soles of his feet so badly? (Jon shuddered a bit at remembering the feeling -- fuck did it tickle.) Jon was trying to piece things together, but the whole bizarre universe of sensations he had experienced over the past whenever -- how long has he been in this predicament, again? -- was leaving his brain disorganized and jumbled. He had almost completely forgotten about Sandra, far more concerned about his current scenario and for good reason.

Yet Jon didn't have time to think about his situation too much, as the glass door in front of him slid open, and a young black guy entered. He had a bit of a fro, pearly-white teeth, a gray T-shirt with a logo on the front that Jon didn't recognize, dark-blue jeans, and a nice pair of white trainers. The young man -- who Jon had to guess was in his early 20s -- seemed upbeat, pretty happy. He immediately knelt down to face Jon, who leaned back into a kneeling position so the two were about eye-level. Already, being tied and naked in front of such a "regular" guy started really ramping up the embarrassment factor inside Jon once again.

"Hi there, Jon," the young man started. "My name is Jason."

"Um ... hi?" Jon said, unsure of what to make of this.

"Ha, yes, a good ol'-fashioned hello would do it," Jason stated, smiling. "Anyways, I'm here as your personal trainer. I'm going to get you ready and prepped for your new master. Once we've achieved 100% compliance, you'll be able to move around the premises and serve just like any of the other good acquisitions will be able to, only to return to your cell every night. I know it doesn't sound like much, but trust me, it is a world of difference."

"What ... what the fuck are you talking about, man?" pleaded Jon, horribly confused.

"Jeez," Jason said, somewhat dismissively, "you really haven't figured it out yet? Well lemme break it down for you: your old life is gone, boy. You belong here now, and you're going to stay here until you're no longer needed, which, given your handsome looks, I'm guessing won't be for a decade or two."

"So what am I doing here?"

"Well," started Jason, "you're here to be played with. You're a tickleslave, Jon, and you're going to be tickled day in and day out for years on end. If you hate tickling -- which, from what I've read up on, seems to be your case -- then I recommend you learn to love it pretty quickly, because you're going to be getting a lot of it in a very short amount of time, starting with me."

At this point, Jason stood up and casually walked over to the control panel near the entrance of Jon's cell and pressed a few buttons. Just as Jon feared, he could see the metal chain that his wristcuffs were attached to slowly get pulled up through the hole in the ceiling. The process was very slow, which meant Jon was going to be suspended soon, likely at a 45 degree angle just as before. Jon struggled a bit, but even that was a bit subconscious: he knew he didn't have much of a say in what was about to happen. In fact, he didn't have any say at all.

"So here's what we got to get you to do, Jon," started Jason as he watched the boy's nude body get slowly taught. "We're going to achieve 100% compliance. What is that you might ask? Well, it's simple man: you're going to love being tickled so much you're going to ask me to tickle you. On your own volition. On your own free will. You're going to love tickling, and request that anyone who is even remotely higher up the chain than you give you a tickle session worth having."

Jon was now fully taught, suspended by chains and cuffs, at a 45 degree angle, spread out in a reverse-Y like he was some midair flesh kite. His toes were about a foot off the ground now, and boy did they stretch to try and reach it. His arms were *very* secure over his head, leaving his armpits far too exposed and vulnerable for his comfort.

Jon suddenly got a bit defiant: "Well listen here Jason, you can tickle me for weeks on end but there is no humanly possible way that I'm going to enjoy being tickled. Not now, not ever. You're running a fool's errand."

Jason burst into laughter. "Dude, wow. Jon ... you're funny!" He approached Jon, standing inches away from the boy's suspended face, smirking. "You know, every single person that comes in here says some sort of deviation of what you just said just now." Jason outstretched his index finger and began tracing circles in Jon's plump belly. Jon bit his lip instantaneously, trying to avoid a reaction. "You know how this plays out, Jonny Boy? You give in. You have literally no choice but to give in. I mean, what else are you going to do: be defiant and continued to be tickled against your will for months on end? For a year?" Jon let out little fits of laughter, but his face was still distorted in a defiant grimace. "Everyone submits in the end, boy. There's no shame in it. Although, if you *want* to keep being defiant, you're going to make my year, Jon." At this point, Jason's index fingers were teasing and prodding Jon's protruding nipples, causing Jon to tilt his head back, fighting what his nerves were telling him to do. "So please, let's begin, and although submitting to your fate is the easiest way out, please don't. Please fight for as long as possible, because I'm going to enjoy the living hell out of this."

With that, Jason's fingers jumped right into Jon's armpits, and the boy let out high-pitched scream, his small defenses completely shattered. Jason wasn't a "nice" or "easy" tickler -- he was venomous. His fingers dived, scraped, and poked at a rapid, unrelenting pace, and immediately Jon began swinging back and forth in his suspended state. Jon laughed like a hyena, Jason's prodding of this pits were nothing short of expert-like. Jason quickly honed in on a soft spot that seemed to make Jon laugh on command, and within seconds, Jon began pleading between bellows of laughter. "Please!" he cried. "Please stop tickling me!" Jason relished this.

"What's that boy? You *want* me to keep tickling you?" Jason said, fingers ablaze.

"Noooo!" Jon cried out. "Please *stop* tickling me!" He drowned himself out with laughter.

"Oh, isn't that cute," started Jason, continuing to destroy the boy's tender pits. "Our tickletoy doesn't want to be tickled no more. Too bad he tickles so well, 'cos that means he's gonna get a whole bunch of tickles, isn't that right, tickletoy?"

Jon could only spurt laughter in response, wiggling in his restraints and fighting all that he could, but to so little avail. Jason tickled and tickled and tickled. Before long, Jason took his tongue to one of Jon's nipples and began to lap at it while he continued tickling the daylights out of Jon. "Mmm, tastes so tender," Jason remarked. His tickling fingers stopped ever so briefly to refocus their attention on Jon's nipples, licking and fondling and toying with the boy. Jon, delirious with laughter, could barely focus on the sensations that were afflicting him at the moment, but suddenly he felt something attach to his ... oh no, it couldn't be.

Yes, so distracted by his tickle-fried body, Jon failed to notice that Jason's elaborate nipple play had managed to conjure an erection out of him, and Jason somehow attached to his manhood was a device that felt remarkably similar to the one Gustav attached to him earlier. Just as before, with the flick of a switch, it began pumping away on his horny, throbbing cock. Jon's look of terror immediately locked in with Jason's smirking gaze.

"Please," Jon pleaded, "turn it off!"

"I don't think so," said Jason, casually, playing with his food. "I think given how hard you are right now, you actually like being played with."

"No, you don't understand," Jon said, clearly trying to fight the erotic sensations that were coursing through his cock, "I can't cum like this again. It's too intense. I literally can't take it."

"OK," said Jason. "Then what are you going to do for me if I take it off you?"

"Guh!" groaned Jon, those two metal rings getting another long pump out of him. "Anything. Please for the love of fuck I'll do anything!"

"Like ..."

"Like what?" said Jon, more desperate.

"Like begging me to tickle you more?"

"No!" screamed Jon, the intensity building up within him, entirely against his will. "I can't! I fucking hate being tickled!"

"Well then," said Jason, "looks like I'm just going to have to tickle you after you cum."

"Nooooo!" screamed Jon, wiggling and tugging at his restraints, swaying a bit while doing nothing to prevent the device from wailing away, pumping and pumping his shaft over and over again. His hips began bucking uncontrollably, the base of his shaft began pumping, getting ready for the inevitable explosion.

"Now this is my favorite part," smirked Jason.

"Ahhhhhhh!" Jon screamed, and with that, gobs upon gobs of semen came firing out of him, one load after another after another. Jon's arms seizured every once in a while trying to release the sensations that were coursing through his body. Of course, even as his shots started to dissipate, the device attached to his member continued to pump at random intervals, and Jon level of speech was reduced down to that of a drooling idiot.

"Please," he pleaded, weakly, to Jason. "Turn it off. I ... I can't take."

"You can't what?" said Jason, playing with his food again.

Jon shuddered with the latest pump. "Please take it off. I'm ... I can't."

"What?"

Another pump of oversensitive pleasure. Jon suddenly began to cry, helpless. "Please! Just ... please!"

Jason walked over to the helpless boy and flicked the switch off, slowly and carefully removing the device while observing Jon's tears of sexual anguish slowly streaked down his face. Jason stood right in front of the sagging tickle toy, his face suddenly sympathetic.

"Jon," he started, "is this too much for you?"

Jon, proud as he could between his voice breaking, said "Yes. It's ... way too much."

"I'm sorry, Jon," said Jason. "'cos you ain't seen nothing yet."

Jason's fingers dug right into that sweet spot in Jon's armpits, and he let out the most desperate, throat-shredding yelp he had ever given in his life. Little did Jon realize at this moment that he still had hours and hours and hours of torture to go.

+ + +

After another day's exhaustive work, Jon was returned to his resting room. It was an unusual room to be sure, made of dark brown stone, and "room" didn't really do it justice. It was more of a box built into a wall, and just like every other place he had been in since his ordeal started, he was facing a glass panel. Yet now that he was -- as far as he could keep track -- in Day Three of his experience with Jason, his knew the routine: as soon as an armed guard carried his lifeless, exhausted-from-tickling body back to the cell, he had to go and place his feet within the two holes at the base of that glass window. The guard then pressed a button that locked them in place, and Jon could sit in this box -- no wider than a study desk -- with a full range of motion. Food could be delivered, water was available via a plastic tube that was threaded in to his room, but his feet remained waist-level in another room on the other side of this glass. On either side of him was dark brick walls that were firmly in place. Jon couldn't see much, but he could see that much as with the U-shaped "auction" room he was a part of however long ago, there was someone facing him across the way, his body and shape in a familiar predicament. From what Jon could see, there were guys on the either side of him, and his best guess was that there were two rows of guys in glass cells, their feet sticking out into a hallway. Occasionally a guard would walk by through the hallway, but so far, even though Jon's soft soles were exposed and helpless on the other side of the glass, nothing was going to be done to them. So far, the guy from across the way seemed to be groggy or completely passed out every time Jon looked over -- the two hadn't made eye contact even some three days in. Unable to do anything given his feet were locked in, Jon simply laid back on his elbows and looked up at the faint bulb that lit him, wondering how much time has passed since his ordeal began.

An hour passed as Jon stared up at the ceiling, lost in thought, piecing ideas and plans and theories together about what to do about his predicament, and avoiding thoughts about tickling at any possible cost. It was hard work, and his body and mind already felt completely worn out from what he had gone through. Jon now laid flat on his back, curled his toes on the other side of the glass, and started to drift to sleep.

"Hey."

Jon's eyes opened. He looked around -- there was nothing there.

"Hey you."

Jon heard a voice coming from his ... right? But there was a wall there. How could--

"There's a small crack. Bit of a hole. Fifth row of bricks up, about the middle."

Jon looked at where the voice was directing him and saw the same crack as well as, yes, an absolutely minute hole. He leaned in as far as he could and, to his surprise, saw another eyeball staring at him from the other side.

"Hello?" Jon said, curious.

"Oh my God. Oh my God! Someone! Someone else! Please don't

tell me you're crazy," the voice implored.

"Um, no, just really tired," said Jon, a bit hesitant. "My name's Jon. Who are you?"

"Hello, I'm Jose. How long have you been here, friend? Just a few days, right? At least by my count."

"Yeah, three days."

"Oh man," exclaimed Jose, "hold on to that. Hold on to knowing how many days you've been here. It starts off so easy but you get lost along the way. Horribly, terribly lost. It's ... not easy, as you can imagine."

"How long have you been here?" Jon asked.

"Oh lord," started Jose. "I lost track awhile ago, but I'd say about three years or so. It is just a constant nightmare. A tickle nightmare unlike anything else. It is terrifying."

"So what do they do to you?" asked Jon.

"Oh, they tickle you," Jose said, matter of factly. "They tickle you until you can't take it anymore and then they tickle you for a few more hours beyond that. They will extract multiple orgasms out of you every single day. If you're lucky, the Master will bring you upstairs and tickle you while worshiping your feet. It's nice because Master isn't all that skilled a tickler but he loves it more than anyone else here."

"The Master?" said Jon, who through the cracks could see that Jose was a nice pale South American man just a few years younger than he was. He could also see that he had somewhat of a Dartanian-styled goatee on his face.

"Yes. Um, forgive me for asking, but you were purchased recently, yes?"

Jon was unsure. "Um, I guess?"

"If you don't know, then yes, you were purchased," explained Jose dryly. "The young man with the sunglasses? That is Master. He is the reason why you're here."

"What?" said Jon, horridly confused.

"Somehow, you got picked up and brought to market because of your ticklishness. Given how it's illegal nowadays, I'm guessing some people just can't get enough of a fix, so there's a black market for guys like you and me: trinkets to be bought and sold like we're currency. In truth, we're just tickleslaves, whose only purpose is to be tickled and teased and tormented for Master's amusement."

Jon was a bit aghast. "That's ... that's what we've become? Tickle currency?"

"Yes," said Jose, "and worship toys. Master loves male feet. Like, a lot. And if he likes yours, he won't stop paying attention to you for weeks on end."

"What do you mean?" asked Jon.

Suddenly, a large metal door could be heard opening. A bit of light flooded the hallway where the two rows of barefoot men faced each other. Jon couldn't see much, but he could see everyone snapping to attention.

"What's going on?" Jon asked.

"*Keep your voice down!*" Jose said in a forceful whisper. "*It seems that Master is high again, taking a trip down Prisoner's Lane.*"

"What?" asked Jon again.

"*He's <u>high</u>,*" said Jose, "*and when he gets high he gets really horny, and he teases and tickles and worships whichever pair of feet he likes the most. My advice is simple: take it and pretend you* *like it.*"

"Boyyyyyyyyyyyyyyyyyyyys!" Jon could hear from the hallway (although amplified -- it appears there was a speaker in his cell that pumped in the Master's voice). "I'm horny, I'm stoned out of my mind, and you all have such wonderful feet tonight!" Jon noticed how he gave a particularly lustful emphasis to the word "feet" -- this guy meant it.

"*Again,*" Jose whispered, "*pretend like you enjoy it.*"

"Now," the Master intoned, his speech occasionally slurred, "who's going to please my tongue the most tonight?"

Jon could hear a cacophony of "Ooh, me! Pick me!"-type hollers from the various prisoners, but Jon just didn't have it in him to fake that kind of enthusiasm. Jon couldn't even see this Master kid from his limited viewpoint.

"Jeremy," the Master said to some poor soul that was outside of Jon's line of vision, "how was your day today?"

"Oh," said the very gawky-sounding Jeremy, still unseen, "Aaron worked me over very hard. He made me into a grand ol' tickle toy, trust me." Jon could hear a bit of trepidation in Jeremy's voice.

"Oh really?" intoned the Master. Jon next heard a bunch of large slurping sounds and Jeremy's halting laughter, clearly fighting off how much he hated whatever was being done to him, which Jon assumed was a healthy amount of foot licking. "Fuck, Jeremy: your soles taste fucking delicious tonight."

"I try my best sir," said Jeremy, the neverousness still audible. "My feet are ... are yours for the taking."

"Mmmm," moaned the Master, "these are fucking great tasting feet. God, I half wanna fuck 'em right now, but I'll give you something even better. Coochie coochie coo ..."

Jon could hear Jeremy just ooze out laughter, fighting each guffaw as it emerged. "Yes, hehe, thank you sir! I enjoy this so much!"

The laughing settled. A tense silence slowly filled the air.

"Really, Jeremy?" asked the Master, suddenly serious. "Do you really enjoy it?"

Clearly lying, Jeremy said "Yes sir! I love it when you suck on my toes and ... and tickle me to the brink of insanity and back. Yes, I love it."

"Jeremy," said the Master, coolly, "you don't have to lie to me. I may run this whole thing but let's be honest: you were ripped from your comfortable life and forced into a sexual servitude completely against your will. You hate being tickled, you had being forced to cum, and yet we do exactly those things to you day in and day out every single day. Tickling, torturing, teasing, milking. Jeremy, just between you and me, do you love it, or -- deep down, in your heart of hearts -- do you wish you could escape here and go back to your old life?"

It appeared that every prisoner held their breath in tandem, awaiting Jeremy's answer.

"God, I can't stand another second in here, sir!" shouted Jeremy, "It's hell! It's torture! If I cum just one more time I might completely lose my mind!"

Silence again. Jon's heart was beating in his chest; for whatever reason, he was absolutely terrified right now.

"Congratulations, boys!" cried out the Master. "It looks like tomorrow we're having another round of Freeplay! Guards, if you wouldn't mind removing Jeremy here, I'd be much obliged. Boys, you all excited for Freeplay?"

Jon could hear scores of prisoners all cheering like their home team just won a championship, all drowning out the sounds of

Jeremy struggling as he was manhandled by some guards, in all likelihood Jon leaned over to the wall and whispered as loud as he could over the ruckus.

"Jose," he asked, *"what's Freeplay?"*

Jose replied: *"Freeplay is when someone who has clearly broke the rules is tied in a large room and tickled and made to cum as many times as possible."*

Jon arched his eyebrow. *"How is that different from any other day?"*

"The difference is that it isn't our keepers who do the tickling. It's us."

Jon was a bit stunned. *"But, why would we do that?"*

"'cos we're watched as we do it, plus we're good at it." Jose continued, *"Think about it: keepers are told to watch over us and drive us insane and torture us day in and day out. By the end of the day, they're almost as exhausted as we are. Yet when the tables are turned and we're told to go 'full-out' on one of our own, who wouldn't pass up the chance? The ones that are really at tickling our own are sometimes called out to higher duties, some even ascending to the level of keeper. It's our only way out of here, even if it leads to a dead end."*

Jon mulled this over as the hooting and hollering slowly died down. The Master was making his way down the hallway.

"I know boys," he said, "it's an exciting day, but I still haven't busted my nut over any of your sweet tootsies yet, and boy do I want to." Jon could hear the footsteps drawing closer to where he was.

"Jose!" the Master exclaimed, "how are you doing today?"

"Ticklish as always, sir!" Jose exclaimed, faking enthusiasm like a pro.

"You want me to tickle your feet a bit?" said the dominant horndog.

"Yes, there is nothing I'd like more!" With that, Jon didn't hear Jose laugh: he was actually giggling. Giggling helplessly as the Master tickled him, Jose totally helpless to the feeling. "Ahhh!" he screamed. "It tickles so much!"

"And you like that, right?" asked the Master.

"More than anything in the world, sir!" Jose said before giggling sweetly again.

"Very nice," said the Master as Jose's giggles subsided. "Very nice."

Two steps more and suddenly the Master's face was right in the middle of Jon's view.

"Why hello there, new meat," said the Master, his short brown hair all over the place, those same damn white-rimmed sunglasses on, a necklace made of puka shells around his neck, some yellow T-shirt donned (Jon couldn't see anything below that). "What's your name?"

Jon was nervous but was trying to play cool. "Jon. My name is Jon."

The Master tilted his head, trying to recognize him. He was obviously intoxicated, unable to connect thoughts. Then it hit: "AH! Jon! Yes. The one I spent an absolutely ludicrous amount of money on. Yes, how are you Jon?"

"Good," Jon lied, "tired. Really exhausted from all of this tickling."

"Oh really?" said the Master. "You don't like being tickled?"

"No," said Jon, ignoring all of Jose's warnings, "but I don't really have much of a say in the matter, so I guess I'm going to have to learn to like it, right?"

"Yes," the Master said, "that was a very good response. You are correct: you are going to learn to like it quite a bit." He smirked. "Jon, answer me a question though: how tasty are your toes?"

"I'm not quite sure, sir," Jon said, somewhat to his own amazement, "but I guess the best way to find out is to try them yourself."

"Mmm," the Master moaned, "I guess you're right." With that, the Master's face seemed to slam into Jon's right sole like a magnet, and immediately his tongue, his teeth, and the rest of his mouth engorged, lapped at, and tickled Jon's naked feet. Jon yelped again as the Master's right hand grabbed Jon's left foot to steady himself (and to fondle a bit, Jon presumed) so he could focus his oral activities on Jon's right foot. The Master's tongue lazily dabbed different areas of Jon's sole: the instep, the toepads, the heel, the sides -- clearly this kid was relishing the experience. Jon's laughter came in halting waves, always peaking whenever Master's teeth dug into his arch and began to drag down, tickling along the way. Jon could hear the Master unzipping his pants and could see the Master's right arm reach down and start to wail away on his own erection. The Master's tongue now seemed intent to prod the areas between Jon's toes, and fuck did that tickle, slurping and slithering in-between Jon's intimate areas. "Yeah, you like that don't you?" the Master said lustfully.

Jon could barely keep it together, but managed to blurt out one sentence: "I bet these toes taste fucking great don't they?"

Suddenly, the Master's moans went up an octave, and with a few more jacking gestures, seemed to shoot his load against the wall underneath where Jon's right foot was. A few aftershock moans came through as the Master seemed to be frozen, collecting himself. After a moment, he stood up straight and zipped his pants back up. It took him a moment to compose himself, but the Master was clearly satisfied about what just transpired. He looked up to Jon directly (or at least Jon thought he did, given the sunglasses), and was blunt: "Jon, I think you're going to do very well here. I'll be keeping my eye on you ... and your feet." Again, "feet" was emphasized very prominently.

"And with that," the Master announced out loud, "I wish you all a wonderful night! Feet dreams!"

The Master's footsteps echoed out, getting farther and farther from where Jon could hear them. Then, the giant metal door could be heard shutting. The overhead lights went several shades dimmer -- implied nighttime.

"What the hell was that?" Jose asked through the crack in the wall.

Jon looked over at the eyeball burning a hole through him in the crack, replying "Honestly? I don't know. Whatever it was though, it worked."

Jose didn't say anything to Jon for the rest of the night.

+ + +

The next morning, Jon was pulled out of his cell by a large, muscled guard, as per what has become the routine. Jon was still groggy but was again being forcibly lead by the hand down more hallways of white walls and florescent lights, a few doors visible but all of them marked with metallic button panels that controlled entry and exit. The rooms with actual doors didn't concern Jon: it was the rooms with large glass fronts that did, as those were the places where things happened; terrible, ticklish things.

As fate would have it, Jon was being lead to one of these rooms, but it was a much larger room, and two of its four walls were glass. Jon looked at the surrounding rooms and gathered that this two-glass room must be some sort of communal area between all the individual "keeper" rooms. Jon could also see that there were a half-dozen prisoners already inside, completely nude, just like him.

They all seemed to be of the same type: thin-to-average build, scruffy hair, a few with some tattoos on them, all of them at the moment with their heads down, as if trying to ignore whatever was going on. Jon's guard pressed some buttons on the key panel and the glass door slid open, and Jon was lightly shoved into the room. Before closing the door, the guard said one thing to him: "No socializing."

Jon was now standing naked in a room of some guys who looked the same with the explicit instruction not to talk -- no wonder all their heads were downcast: they didn't want to risk any social interaction to speak of (Jon assumed that the punishment for doing so was ... well, he knew full well by now what that was).

Minutes passed, and every so often, a guard would drop by yet another prisoner. Eventually, Jose was dropped off, and after being told "no socializing" by his guard, he sat down next to Jon, who was standing with his back up against the wall. Jon just stood there, unsure of what to think, but managed to hear something just barely:

"*Speak very, very quietly. Barely move your lips.*"

Jon followed suit, as quiet as a mouse, trying to be a ventriloquist: "*What's going on?*"

"*Freeplay.*"

"*So ...*" Jon started, "*we just tickle the shit out of him?*"

"*Or,*" Jose said firmly, "*you don't do anything. As crazy as it is, you'll know who got you and who didn't. They don't punish you for sitting out, but it's best to build up as much goodwill as you can, because if it's your turn, you'll want as many friends on your side as possible.*"

Suddenly, some whirring mechanics behind the wall got into motion, and a giant panel slowly rotated around like a trick bookshelf. On the other side was Jeremy, a guy who looked no younger than 18, lanky, blond surfer hair, unmistakably weak judging by his muscle tone. He was restrained flat against the wall by these intense-looking metallic locks, and yes, he was completely naked. He already looked worn out, as if he had been "warmed up" by some keepers earlier.

"Hey boyyyyyyyyys!" The Master over the loudspeaker. "You know what time it is?"

Every man in the room aside from Jon & Jose called out in unison: "Freeplay!"

"That's right! And we all know the rules right? Make Jeremy here regret having any free thoughts of his own -- the only way we know how."

And with that, the gang of boys all gathered around Jeremy's bound, helpless body, and they went crazy: poking, prodding, scraping, squeezing, and tickling every inch of flesh they could get their eager hands on. Jon was a bit taken back the intensity of the other prisoners: after having had to take it for so long, they must *really* want to dish out the same. Jon could only describe it as animal-like, and could only describe Jeremy as helpless. The boy's head shook wildly back and forth as it tried to comprehend the torture that was being inflicted upon it, but absolutely zero mercy was being shown. It wasn't some five minutes in until he began to sprout tears. God, Jon knew what that boy was going through -- then again, so did everyone else in this room.

Jon felt almost helpless, as he wanted to really help the kid, but the rest of the guys were positively unleashed at this moment, dragging countless fingernails across his soles, wiggling hands into his armpits, squeezing his inner thighs while poking his ribcage with a dozen fingers. Jon thought he had it bad with Jason, but the truth was that Jeremy was the one going through tickle hell right now.

About 20 minutes in to the non-stop onslaught, Jon noticed that on the glass wall opposite Jeremy, the Master and two bodyguards had showed up at some point and were watching intently. Undoubtedly they saw Jon & Jose not participating, but their focus seemed to be entirely on watching Jeremy's soul bend and snap. Over the course of the next 20 minutes, some of the prisoner's heads would turn to notice that the Master was watching, but realizing this only made them tickle Jeremy harder, and there seemed to be no more octaves for Jeremy's brittle, crackling voice to reach. Jon continued to stare at Jeremy's tickle abuse intently, while Jose remained sitting on the ground, his head down, almost as if he were wishing for this whole thing to go away.

Eventually, once Jon estimated they had reached the hour mark, the glass door entrance to this room slid open, and all the boys instantaneously stopped and parted to opposite sides of the room -- completely silent while they did so -- giving the Master a direct view of Jeremy. Jon was a bit stunned by what he saw: Jeremy's entire body was a light shade of sunburn red, every single inch of him having been worked over a couple thousand times in the course of that hour. Sweat positively dripped off of him, his lungs panting so heavy that he could be mistaken for a smoker who just finished a 100m dash. The Master simply grinned.

"You had enough, darling?" he said to Jeremy.

"I ... think ... so," the boy panted out, exhausted.

"And what lesson did we learn?" teased out the Master.

"To ... always ... accept your ... punishment."

"Very good, boy," the Master said. "And very good, boys. I might tell your keepers to keep it to only one orgasm today as a special treat."

At that moment, something totally came over Jon that he had never experienced ever: a defiant impulse. A survival instinct. Something ... fiery. Either way, Jon's bare feet pounded firmly on the floor as he made is way directly over to Jeremy's exhausted body, immediately jabbing his fingers in his sides, causing the boy to yelp.

"No! You're wrong!" shouted Jon, eliciting a gasp from everyone in the room, even the Master. Jon's fingers made a beeline directly towards the boy's pits and he started working on the same sweet spot that Jason gets him at every single day, talking the whole way through: "The lesson isn't to accept your punishment. None of this is punishment: all of this is reward. The Master has brought you hear to give you the gift of tickling and you call it punishment? How dare you treat his generosity as 'punishment'. I oughta tickle the shit out of you all over again."

The boy's sweat-drenched hair flopped back and forth as he laughed, guffawed, and pleaded. "What the fuck are you doing man? Ha ha PLEASE! You're tickling me!"

"That's right, bitch," said Jon. "You never say that you had your fill to the Master. He's the goddamn Master after all. When he asks if you had enough, you say 'No sir, give me more!' even if you can't stomach another second of it." Jon's tongue reached up to the boy's left nipple as Jon's hand played with the right, and slowly he began teasing the boy. "Say, 'I like it when you tickle me, Master.'"

Against all his will, Jeremy sputtered out a sentence, staring at the Master as he spoke: "I .. ha ha! ... like it when you t-t-tickle me, M-Master!"

Jon -- who, it should be noted, was as straight as they come -- immediately went and grabbed Jeremy's half-flaccid penis and began violently jerking, his other hand still teasing Jeremy's nipple while he verbally dominated him, "Yeah, you're getting horny just thinking about Master torturing you later, aren't you?"

Panicked, Jeremy responded "Yes, yes I can't wait!"

Jon kept at it, jerking the boy away even as every single impulse told him not to, and after less than a minute, the boy let out a very weak, small cum shot, no doubt worn down because of the hour of unrelenting tickle torture he had just experienced. Jon finished by saying "Remember that for next time, bitch!" before turning and facing the entrance.

Jon saw nothing but a sea of faces, jaws totally agape, the Master smiling. In fact, the Master began a slow clap, spacing out his applause dramatically, and the rest of the guys soon awkwardly, slowly joined in.

"Well," the Master started, walking towards Jon, "I don't know what the hell that was ... but I liked it." He pointed to all the prisoners at once while placing his arm on Jon's shoulder: "All of you pay attention. This man took a risk, but I think it paid off wonderfully -- don't you, Jeremy?"

Jeremy's exhausted head lifted up, and he spoke faintly: "Yes, message received: always, always ask for more tickling."

The Master grinned. "Lesson learned. Good boy." He then turned to Jon. "Who's your keeper again?"

Jon replied flatly: "Jason."

"Oooh, yes," the Master said, "Jason is one of our best. I'll make sure to pay particular attention to your session today." He then gestured broadly to the room. "I hope you got all of your aggression out of your systems boys, as your guards will be coming by to pick you up one by one and take you to your respective keepers." He then began to exit the room. "Ta ta for now, my tickletoys!"

He walked with his guards in tow as the glass door slid shut behind him. One by one, other guards came by to valet the boys back to their keepers, the entire room silent as per the no socialization guidelines laid out earlier. However, each time one walked by Jon, they gave him a dirty look, as if Jon had done something wrong to curry favor with the Master. Either way, Jon didn't have much time to process whatever shade they were throwing at him. He was still getting over the fact that for the first time in his life he touched another man's penis, much less jacked him off. The experience was interesting, but Jon was still straight: it wasn't something he wanted to do again, but was something he felt he did out of necessity. Should he ever get out of this place alive, a future therapist will have a field day with this. For now, however, his guard had shown up, and off to another intense session with Jason he went. As he looked back at the partially see-through room, he saw Jose give him a very sad look, as if it was the last time they were going to see each other. Jon had little idea what it meant, but felt that something was in the air -- something very, very different.

+ + +

"Well well well," sneered Jason, gleefully, "looks like the star of Freeplay has decided to join us." Jon's bare feet slapped quietly against the floor as his guard led him into Jason's glass room. This was new for Jon, as he's usually not escorted here: he's either gassed unconscious or passes out from exhaustion before he appears in a new location. The guard shoved Jon in the room, but the glass door didn't slide close yet. Jon surmised that the guard was waiting for Jon to get in restraints before he would leave. Jon started out nervous, but his discomfort grew exponentially when he saw his usual suspension setup was nowhere to be seen. Instead, Jason was standing next to waist-high table that appeared five feet long and less than two feet wide. On either side of this was a large, curved metal plate, and it appeared each side could rise up and latch into each other, creating a metal cocoon for ... whoever was stuck inside. Jon sighed, realized what his fate would be.

"So I take it you're tickling me hot-dog style today?" bemoaned Jon to Jason, wearing a black T-shirt today with the rest of his getup the same as usual.

"Yes," said Jason, smiling. "Orders from above say we got to try something new on you today."

Jon went over and lied down on the table, but there wasn't enough room for him to fit entirely. There was an elevated white foam pillow which was obviously where his head was to rest, but his feet still hung off the edge by a substantial-- oh, that's the game we're playing.

"Arms by your side, boy," ordered Jason, and Jon obliged, realizing that resistance, truly, was futile. Jason then pressed a button on the control panel on the wall and the two curved metal plates slowly rose up and clasped together, trapping Jon's naked body underneath, looking like a silver mummy tomb with the head and feet completely visible and vulnerable. Jon couldn't help but note how utterly snug his entrapment felt, and was sure he would be sweating through this in virtually no time at all. His feet wiggled a bit, completely helpless. At this point, Jon could see that the glass door had closed and the guard was gone -- it was just him and Jason now.

Jason walked over and began stroking his hand along Jon's forehead, tenderly pushing his hair back. "Jon," Jason started, "you really are a beautiful, handsome man. You probably wouldn't think of yourself as sexy, but damn boy: you're a little taste of something wonderful. My favorite specimen by far."

"Would hate to disappoint," Jon dryly quipped.

"Oh trust me, you've done better than half of the other schlubs out here. I'd put you in the top 10%." Jason leaned over and whispered in Jon's ear: "Just between you and me, I don't think I've ever seen the Master take a shining to someone so quickly. Play your cards right and you can be out of here in a week."

Jason stood back up, seeming to ignore that the boys' secret conversation even happened.

"Now," Jason declared, "on a scale of one to ticklefuck, how ticklish are your bare, vulnerable feet, Jon?"

"Oh, I don't know," Jon said, playing along, "I'd say about a 7 or so."

Jason smirked. "You're a funny guy, Jon." Jason moved himself around so he was kneeling directly in front of Jon's feet, placing his hands along the heels and sides, feeling them. "It's just a shame that your best laugh line is the one I'm about to draw in your foot."

Jon's eyes closed and preemptively grimaced, expecting the worst. Five seconds passed and nothing happened. Then ten. Then ten more. Jon half-opened his right eyelid to look around, and Jason was just staring at him, soon bursting out into laughter. "Oh man," he said, "you're making this too fun, Jon. Your feet must be ticklish as *fuck* if you're prepping for something like that already."

'Well," Jon started, nervously, "I did say they were about a 7."

"No no no, Jon," said Jason, playfully, "even without tickling them, I don't think your feet are a 7, no. In fact, I think they're a hell of a lot closer to *ticklefuck* ..."

With that, Jason's fingernails pounced on Jon's soles, scraping up and down each sole at blazing speed. The ferocity of the attack took Jon completely off guard. "FUCK!" Jon screamed before his hearty laugh came hurtling back to his throat. There was something weird about being contained in a silver tickle tube like this: because his arms were tightly at his side, it didn't feel like Jon was getting the full expansion of his lungs, and his breaths were a bit quicker than usual, more desperate

"Do you got ticklish feet Jon? Do you like it when I take my hands and scrape my fingernails across your bare, helpless, ticklish feet?"

"Fh-uh-ukk!" was about all Jon could muster in response. Jason was going at 100% full-stop without stopping. He was scraping up and down Jon's soles so ferociously it felt as if Jason was actually reaching the inside of Jon's soul in the process. Jon felt like his feet were on fire, and as much as his toes wiggled, stretched, and squirmed, they could not escape Jason's devilish fingers.

"C'mon, boy," he taunted, "laugh for me! Laugh like the tickleslut you are! Fuck, you love tickling so much. Hell, you should be paying me for giving you exactly what you want, ain't that right ticklebitch? Does ticklebitch like being tickled?"

Jon's head turned back and forth and back and forth -- he literally couldn't take it anymore. His shortened breaths were making him go completely red in the face, as his lungs couldn't keep up with the primal, sweaty laughter that Jason was conjuring out of the boy's pink arches.

"Please!" Jon screamed between choked laughter. "I'm ... haHA! ... gonna -- passout!"

"What?" said Jason, slowing only momentarily.

"Gonna," Jon took a giant gulp of air, "gonna passout!"

Jason looked up intently at Jon's face. "No shit, son." Jason stopped his tickling and walked over to where Jon's face was, stroking Jon's forehead just as before, pushing his sweaty brown hair back each time, calming him. "It's OK Jonny Boy. It's OK. It's only tickling. It's OK. You only got several more hours to go."

In truth, Jon's brain was completely blocking out Jason's soothing tone. All it was concerned about was how fucking exhausted he felt after only 20 minutes of tickling. Now a few days in, Jon's entire nervous system was about to hit an exhaustion wall. As much as Jon didn't want to believe it, he had to admit that by the end of today or maybe tomorrow, his spirit would be completely broken. He hated being tickled to start with, but this was all too much: total sensory overload all the time always. Jon simply didn't have the strength in him to survive. Yet, at the same time, he knew that he couldn't do much to prevent what was happening ...

... at which point, Jon had a gigantic revelation.

He was going to be tickled no matter what, but it's better when you're the favorite, as the favorite always gets special treatment in some way or another. Jon's only way out wasn't resigning to his fate, it was taking hold of it. That little voice that told him to dominate Jeremy earlier must've been his subconscious pushing him in the right direction. Admittedly, Jon never wanted to touch another man's cock again for as long as he lived, but if doing things like that made him the apple of the Master's eye, then so be it: the only way out was through. Jon had to turn up the charm, flirt with everyone who came in eye contact with him, and -- worst of all -- actually pretend like he enjoyed being tickled. Jon swallowed his pride and his humility one last time, because he was going to throw it all out the window.

"Do you need some water?" asked Jason somewhat playfully but with an undertone of actual sincerity. Jason didn't wait for an answer, but simply walked up to what was no doubt some hidden panel containing water bottles in the wall (Jon assumed), but Jon wasn't having it.

"Who's the water for: me or you?" Jon blurt out.

Jason turned around sharply. "Come again, boy?"

"I was under in the impression that you enjoyed tickling," Jon said, "and you're taking a break after 20 minutes?"

"I'm sorry," Jason started, walking over to Jon's exposed feet, "but I was under the impression that just a few moments ago, you were the one begging for me to stop because you were about to pass out."

"Oh c'mon," Jon said, sweat still on his brow, "that was just for show. Besides, we all know what's going on here, really."

"What?" Jason said, intrigued.

"You're not here to tickle me, dude. I'm here for the sole purpose of being tickled by you. I came here to experience your talent, and boy you did not disappoint."

Jason hopped up to sit on the metal shell Jon was trapped under, sitting right near Jon's feet, Jason's legs swung to one side, his right hand hanging perilously close to Jon's plump, naked toes.

"So, what you're saying," Jason started, "is that you came all the way here to meet me?"

"Tickling's illegal," Jon noted, "and for good reason. And when something is wrong or illegal, one outlaw always comes to the forefront. You may not know this, but Jason -- your name is legendary."

Jason's eyebrow arched, unsure if Jon was telling the truth or was totally bullshitting him. "Really? I'm legendary?"

"Yeah," Jon said. "I mean, you're not walking down red carpets to movie premieres, but you got recognition, and I must say, I'm disappointed in you right now."

Jason was aghast. "Disappointed? The fuck you on about?"

"Look at my toes," Jon said. "Just look at them."

Jason turned his head around to look at the tops of Jon's toes.

"Sexy, right?" Jon teased, wiggling them slightly.

"I mean, a bit yeah ..."

"You're not looking, Jason." Jon was enjoying playing with *his* food. "It's all about the details. Look at my pinkie toe, how it's just so adorably shorter than the rest. Look at how well trimmed my toenails are -- god, they're sexy, aren't they? Look at how rounded and plump they are from underneath. Oh they're just screaming for a mouth to suck all of the flavor right out of them -- or perhaps they're just looking for the right fingers to tickle them. God, just looking at how helpless they are turns you on, doesn't it, Jason?"

Jason, his mouth a bit agape, said "Um, yes, just ... totally."

"C'mon, Jason. Tickle my bare, exposed feet. I know you want to."

Jason hopped down and knelt right in from of Jon's feet again,

Jon's warm soles inches away from Jason's face.

"Jon, you're asking for a world of hurt," Jason warned.

"Only a world?" Jon intoned (nervous as fuck on the inside). "You better be planning to give me more than that.

"You asked for it ..."

Jason was nanoseconds away from attacking Jon's soles with animal ferocity when suddenly both heard the loud, booming word: "STOP!"

Both boys turned and faced the glass front of their room, completely oblivious to the fact that the door had slid open. There stood the Master with two guards behind him, smirking as always. Jason immediately stood straight up like he was at attention in the military.

"I'm sorry sir," Jason spurted out. "I had no idea you were here."

"Oh, I don't blame you," the Master said, walking slowly towards Jon's helpless tootsies. "How could you not be intrigued by feet such as these? So tender, so helpless ..." The master brushed his hands across both Jon's soles in one swoop, causing Jon's mouth to clench a bit. The Master walked closer to Jon. "Boy, are you enjoying yourself?"

Jon was surprisingly nervous, but answered in character: "Not really -- I'm not even being tickled right now."

The Master's smile positively lit up. "Ooh, that's what I like to hear. Between your sessions with Jason so far today and your wonderful dominance around Jeremy earlier, I can't help but wonder: what's going on with you, sweet Jonathan?" The Master ran his fingers through Jon's messy hair (why was everyone suddenly doing that, Jon thought). "What could possibly be going on in that big sexy brain of yours that's making you hold my attention the way that you're doing?"

"You're the Master, right?" Jon asked. "I'm here to serve the Master."

The Master grinned again, and stood straight up. He turned to face his three employees, all of whom looked at the Master with great intent.

"Boys," the Master began, "here's what we're going to do. I usually wait a bit longer before jumping into things, but this is probably the one time I'd be willing to make an exception. As you know, I'm having a wonderful dinner party tomorrow night with some of my dearest friends, and I could use a new toy to show off like this. Thus, as of tomorrow morning, clear out Jon's cell and promote him to Houseboy." The Master turned to Jon, "Trust me, with feet like that, you're going to enjoy it."

Without further statement, the Master began walking towards his guards waiting outside the glass door. Jason spoke before the moment passed: "But sir!" The Master turned to face his employee. "What shall I do with Jon until tomorrow?"

The Master smirked. "Make him pass out, of course."

The glass door slid shut and the Master and his guards were out of view. Jason turned back to Jon, smiling the most devious of smiles. "You heard what the boss said."

Jon's heart beat faster and faster, dreading the next few hours. Lying through his teeth, he looked Jason dead in the eye and simply said "Bring it."

Jon didn't last two hours before falling unconscious.

+ + +

When Jon awoke, he was lying on ... an old bench? He must've been resting on his side, but it felt like days had passed. He looked around: he was in a room made of white tile, but there were very small, barred windows and a (apparently locked) olde wooden door of yore. Jon stood up, only to find something else very unusual: he was wearing a very fancy tuxedo vest. White shirt, black vest, bow tie, jet-black dress pants, and -- no shoes. If he had shoes on, he could go to the opera right now, but with the white sleeves and black vest, he looked more like ... a waiter, he guessed? No matter, he stood up on the vent to look out the window. He couldn't see much (it was high enough he couldn't see the ground below), but he could make out trees, a setting sun coloring the sky a fiery yellow, and the occasional sound of birds. He couldn't tell if he was in the woods or on a private estate or anything, but he was certainly somewhere.

Something else felt weird. Standing on this bench, his feet felt ... sensitive. Soft. Not tickled-to-exhaustion sensitive (although they did still tingle), but something different. He went back to sitting on the bench and rested his left foot on it as well, examining it. His feet never looked so pink, so proper. His toenails were perfectly shaped and rounded, his few toe hairs immaculately groomed. It's as if between Jason tickling him to his breaking point and ... whatever evening he was in right now, his toes had been given the most professional pedicure he had ever seen. Jon continued staring at his own toes: he didn't have a foot fetish, but damn did his size 10s look good. Whatever was happening, someone wanted him presentable.

Suddenly Jon heard the jostling of iron keys in the old wooden door to his room. After some fidgeting, the door swung open and Jon saw a man around his own age dressed very similarly to him: about 6', dressed to the nines, and -- of course -- not wearing shoes. The man had a blond hair in somewhat of a bowl cut, his oval face specked with beardfuzz. The man, gravely in voice but pointed in tone, addressed Jon directly:

"Jon. You're up. Good. Now come here and get ready."

The man walked away, and Jon, confused, set his bare soles on the tile floor and proceeded to walk in the man's direction. Just a few steps out of the door and already Jon was in the middle of an absolutely madcap kitchen: giant wooden table in the middle of the room (seemingly made out of the same material as the door, Jon noted), numerous pots and pans emitting steam and flame, and about a dozen or so people bustling in and out. The chefs were all almost cartoon archetypes: all somewhat portly, black pants, white shirt and apron, numerous chef's hats, and all of them -- wearing shiny black dress shoes. Numerous waiter-like men dressed as Jon was -- all thin, in their 20s, most of them with that same beard shadow that the man who opened Jon's door had -- went in and out, darting around like a hive of bees, each grabbing plates, bottles of wine, champagne glasses, you name it. Jon's eyes widened a bit simply taking in all of this all at once. The man who opened the door grabbed Jon by the shoulder and drew him to a more sequestered area where bottles of wine were stacked up in elaborate wooden racks, still within eyeshot of the main cooking area.

"OK Jon," the gravel-voiced man started, "I need to ask you a few questions."

"Who are you?" Jon asked. "Where the hell am I?"

The man seemed pained to have to answer such simple inquiries. "My name is Aaron, and I'm the head waiter here. You're in the Master's kitchen and you're going to be spending a large amount of time in the main guest room."

"Um, OK," Jon spoke, accepting the reality of this bizarre situation. "You got no shoes on."

Aaron rolled his eyes. "You're a quick one aren't you? Yes, you have no shoes on. None of the servants do. You've been here how long and haven't figured out that the Master has an overwhelmingly powerful male foot fetish?"

Jon was answering slowly, his brain still processing all of this information. "I mean, yeah, OK, but -- why are there so many of us here."

"Because the Master is hosting a very large get together of many of his contemporaries and you're supposed to stand there, look pretty, and serve wine as needed," Aaron said, anxious. "Now you used to be a frat boy, yes?"

"Um, yeah," said Jon.

"Do you know how to make *basic* drinks. And by basic, of course, I mean things like Screwdrivers, Bloody Mary's, things like that."

"Well, Screwdrivers, yes," Jon said, uneven in his responses, "but as for anything fancier than that, well ..."

Aaron looked genuinely frustrated. "For fuck sake, Jon, do you at least know how to pour a glass of wine and not look totally foolish?"

"Yes," Jon stated. "Yes I do."

Aaron grabbed a small silver plate and placed it Jon's hand, directing it to hold it in his palm like any good waiter would. He then immediately placed a bottle of white wine and two long-stem wine glasses on it.

"OK," Aaron said, as if giving a gameplan in a football huddle. "all you need to do is get out there, smile, and let people look at, fondle, and tickle your feet as needed." Aaron looked down at the tops of Jon's feet. "You got a bit of hair on the top there. The guests are going to like you."

Jon smiled a bit but it subsided as soon as he saw Aaron's serious scowl. "Now if this conversation is any indication of how you're going to act, let me give you two pointers: don't fidget and make as little conversation as possible. If you fill up a wine glass or run out of wine you come right back here and grab more and then go right back out there, you got it?"

"Yes," Jon said, still processing.

"Good," Aaron said, giving Jon a slight push towards the swinging doors that appeared to be the exit of the kitchen. "Now go out there and don't fuck up. Impress them enough and you won't even have to know what the Table is."

"Wha?" Jon said, arching his eyebrows.

Aaron pushed him again. "Jesus fuck, just get out there! Guests are arriving!"

Jon took two steps on his pampered feet before stopping and turning back to Aaron who was about to run off and yell at someone probably.

"Aaron!" he said.

Aaron stopped and looked right at Jon. "What?!" he exclaimed, exasperated.

Jon waved for him to come closer. Aggravated, Aaron did so and got in a tight huddle. Jon spoke: "Real quick: if us ... footservants are given free reign of the compound, what's stopping us from just, ya know, walking out of here?"

Aaron's scowl dropped and he looked at Jon earnestly, speaking in a lower volume: "Jon, there is a guard at every possible entrance you can think of. There are cameras at every point where you don't think there's a guard. They will find you, they will catch you. You think Freeplay is bad? The Master has *machines* underground. Machines that don't stop. They will tickle you until you black out, they will milk you until your cock is screaming in pain, and they will not rest no matter how much you plead. You hate being tickled? Trust me, you won't hate it until you get sent down there, where you will lose your mind forever. I've seen it. Whatever risk you think is worth taking, I assure you, it's not worth it."

Aaron leaned up to straight standing position and addressed Jon a bit more formally: "Besides, as crazy as it is, you eventually wind up liking having your feet licked." Jon looked down at Aaron's own podiacal appendages -- they were rather handsome, that light bit of blond fuzz on the tops and toes. "In fact," Aaron said, "it might even become the highlight of your day. Now get out there! We got guests!"

Aaron walked off, the balls of his feet making very distinct slapping sounds every time they plodded across the tile floor. Jon saw him off, looked at the swinging doors in front of him, and put on his game face. He made it a long way in just a few days, and if he played the game right, who knows -- maybe Jon could be out of here by night's end.

As soon as Jon opened the swinging doors, what he saw stunned him: lavish, dark-gold walls lit by numerous chandeliers positioned two full stories above his head, doorways and buttresses with edged covered in rich wood, various classical paintings (all of men, at least one barefoot in each one) hung all over -- this was intimidating. There were numerous chairs and conversation tables about, a few very-nice standing lamps to be seen, and one C-shaped couch surrounding a very unusual oval-shaped granite table that was about knee-high. Jon saw various other footservants simply standing against walls, unmoving, silver tablets balancing wine glasses and drinks just like Jon had. Jon took a step forward and instantly felt the softest fabric ever brush against his bared foot. He looked down and saw the entire floor was made of extremely soft carpet, dark red, and it fucking *tickled* as Jon walked through it. Oh, this was devious, he thought, but then again, the Master had his fetish down to a T -- there wasn't a detail he forgot about. Jon's eyes darted around the room and found a spot on the wall closest to the granite table and simply placed his back flat against it, trying to "blend in" with the rest of the other servants milling about.

Some large doorways off on the side that lead to a smaller, formal dining room suddenly opened and Jon saw the Master walk out with two hulking bodyguards behind him (the guards, Jon noticed, were wearing shoes). The footservants remained unmoving. Aaron entered from the kitchen with a silver tablet that had -- a bottle of Smirnoff and a can of Red Bull on it? That's odd. He went right up to the Master, who today was donning lighter-than-usual blue jeans, a red T-shirt which had a band name on it (Hot Duck, maybe? Jon couldn't see very well), a dark green beanie, those white-rimmed sunglasses as always, and -- a pair of dark green flip-flops. Apparently the Master had no formal clothes. Aaron speed-walked right up to the Master (which surprised Jon, 'cos *fuck* that carpet must be tickling the daylights out of Aaron's soles right now), and did a slight bow.

"How is the Master this evening?" Aaron asked as he poured some vodka into the small crystal glass on his tablet before adding in the Red Bull.

"Horny as fuck," the Master responded to Aaron, "and stoked as hell for my friends to visit." The Master's head swiveled around, admiring the dozen or so footservants gathered about the room. "Looking nice there, Aaron. If things work out well, might even give you a reward tonight."

"I'd like nothing better, sir," Aaron said in a very regal tone.

"Would you like me to tie you up and suck on your toes? For a few hours?"

Aaron's posture wobbled a bit, as if the news was sending horny shockwaves throughout his body. "Yes," Aaron said, a bit of vulnerability showing in his voice, "I'd like that very much."

The Master smirked. "Then keep it up, boy."

A large clock chime could be heard. The Master's eyes went to a very large set of doors at the opposite end of the room where Jon was standing.

"Is it time? Already?" asked the Master.

"Yes," reported Aaron. "There are approximately 20 of your friends and colleagues already lined up and awaiting you behind that door."

"Then open them!" shouted the Master. "Let these motherfuckers in so we can party!"

With that, the Master grabbed his small glass of vodka & Red Bull and took a heavy swig while the tall doors opened. A variety of men, already in conversation, walked in, all in very formal business suits, not one of them wearing shoes. They all started heading towards the Master, some peeling off to get some wine from the standing footservants at the walls. Jon's own toes clenched a bit due to nerves, but clenching them meant dragging them through the ticklish carpet, so put a stop to that immediately. Some classical music slowly faded up (Jon assumed from some unseen speakers somewhere), barely rising above the volume of conversation but giving the room a great deal of ambiance. Jon's whole experience since arriving at ... wherever this was didn't give him a whole lot of time to pause and think about things, but holy shit did this room reek of money.

Minutes had passed while jovial conversations were had. After about a half-hour, Jon hadn't moved from his spot, but simply was content observing all of these unshod men mull about, carrying on with ample conversation wherein it didn't seem like they had seen each other in months. Jon actively listened for names and occupations to get a clearer picture but could only make out a few things: there was Bill, the newspaper magnate with red hair and a halting kind of laugh; Ryan, some sort of music industry figure in dark blue jeans with a rather square-looking head but attractive frame (although he looked more awkward standing barefoot than most anyone else); J.C., who was some hippie-looking guy with a delightfully awkward laugh whom Jon found out was some type of filmmaker -- the list went on. Standing head and shoulders above everyone else was Pat, who appeared to be some sort of former quarterback type with ink-dark hair and a goatee, looking very at ease in his tan casual suit and his 6'6" frame. Between all of the men, jokes were shared, drinks were consumed, all were having a good time, all except Jon who was doing the best to keep his mind active and away from ideas like "how do I escape from this hell hole?"

Suddenly, the looming Pat walked right on up to Jon and stood there, smiling. Jon guesstimated that Pat was in his early 30s but had a very easy-going demeanor to him. He stood in front of Jon, looked down at Jon's feet, and looked right back up.

"You got some nice toes there, boy," Pat spoke with an everyman tone.

"Why ... why thank you, sir." Jon wasn't one who was accustomed to receiving compliments, much less when they were directed specifically at this feet, which he didn't think much of.

"You're welcome, boy. Maybe we can have some fun later." Jon smiled at the remark but was struck with terror by that sentence, his wine tray starting to tremble ever so slightly. "What kind of wine do we have here, boy?"

Jon still trembled slightly. "Um, it's ... uh ... it's white wine, sir."

Pat laughed and turned to the Master, who was in the middle of a conversation with about three other people. "Hey Will!" Pat shouted from across the room, "Is this guy new or something?"

"Yes," the Master shouted back, "was in the basement only as of yesterday."

"Well he's dumb as shit!" Pat yelled back. The two men shared a jocular laugh while Jon just stood there, nervous. Pat turned to face Jon again. "Alright numbnuts, just pour me a bottle of whatever the hell you have there."

"Yes sir," Jon said, still trembling. Trying to pour a bottle into a glass on a tray that he was holding was harder than he thought, however, and elevating the wine, he missed a bit before getting it in the rim of the long-stem.

"Careful, boy," Pat said, "'cos you don't wanna fuck this up for me. My alcoholism is very important." Was ... was that a joke? Jon wasn't sure.

While Jon had absolutely no idea why he was feeling intimidated by Pat, the man's very "direct" presence was really getting to him, as if Pat was judging Jon's each and every movement. Jon's hand holding the tray continued to tremble, and in trying to balance and compensate, Jon missed the tray altogether, accidentally splashing some bubbly onto Pat's bare feet. Jon looked at Pat in the eyes, completely embarrassed, to which Pat responded with a glare.

"Oh no you didn't, boy."

Jon knelt on the ground and set the tray and bottle on the carpet. "I'm sorry sir," Jon pleaded. "Let me get you a towel to wipe that up." Jon was about to stand but Pat's hand touched Jon's forehead and he immediately pushed Jon back into a full kneeling pose.

"Actually," Pat said, sneeringly, "I think you have everything you need to clean this up right under your nose."

Jon looked around, confusingly. Was Pat referring to Jon's shirtsleeve? He wasn't sure --

"Lick it off, boy," Pat ordered, looming over the footslave. Pat then snapped his fingers in front of Jon's face and pointed down.

Without any say in the matter, Jon's head slowly, shamefully tilted forward, soon taking a full, considered view of Pat's toes. Pat had massive feet that were about size 12 or so, with very long toes and prominent black hair on his tops and toeknuckles. It wasn't overwhelming, but notable. Jon simply stared at Pat's gigantic feet for a moment, unsure of what to make of his situation.

"Hey bitch!" Pat said, "Did I fucking stutter? Lick that wine off right now."

Out of the corner of his eye Jon could see that two or three other guys were now standing nearby, observing the spectacle. The pit of Jon's stomach dropped out, as he's never felt so low or so embarrassed in the course of his entire life. Jon had no choice in the matter, so leaned forward so his face was just an inch above the hairs of Pat's feet. Jon could see where the wine had splashed on the tops, and then fought back his gag reflex. Jon didn't even like his girlfriend's feet all that much, so being forced to do this was placing him over the edge. With no way out, Jon closed his eyes tightly and extended his tongue, slowly licking the top of Pat's right foot, his tastebuds touching the tops of Pat's feet, a bit of hair, and the wine all at once.

"That's right, boy," Pat egged, "keep on licking."

Humiliatingly, Jon's tongue continued to explore the tops of Pat's feet, traveling right up to where Pat's leg hair started and then back to where his tongue almost slid in-between Pat's toes. The wine was almost completely gone now but Pat's feet were shining a bit from the inundation of Jon's saliva. Although Jon couldn't see it, Pat was smiling like hell, enjoying this event. He leaned over, arms behind his back, and addressed Jon directly:

"You enjoying this, bitch?"

Jon stopped licking and arched his head up, looking at Pat's face, expecting an answer. Jon grimaced a bit: that voice in the back of his head -- the same one that told him to take charge of his surroundings to win favor with those who matter, even at the expense of his most basic of dignities -- was screaming at him. This was his chance. This was his opening. Jon fought it so hard, especially after doing the most degrading thing he had ever done, but stretched his face into a slight smile, looked up at Pat and said "Actually, I'm enjoying this quite a bit."

Pat snickered, the corner of his mouth morphing into a sneer. "Well," he started, "if this is what you want, then let me give you more of it." Pat turned around (which Jon was grateful for, as those feet weren't anywhere near his face now) and yelled at the Master. "Hey Will! Is the Table in use tonight?"

"Not yet," the dopey-looking Master shouted back. "Found

someone for it?"

"Oh yes," smiled Pat, "I got someone great."

The Master nodded in agreement, put his fingers high up above his head, and snapped twice. Jon wasn't sure what was happening, but suddenly three of the Master's guards appeared and were heading in Jon's directly. Jon calmly stood up, that fucking carpet still tickling his toes as he did so, and the guards, without hesitation, grabbed on to Jon and picked him up, taking him over to the granite table with the couch around it. Jon struggled a bit (getting on the occasional "c'mon!" and "not so rough!"), but before long, saw why the Table always received such an ominous mention: there were four round, padded holes in the table, spaced out like the "4" side of a die (the ones not facing the couch just a little bit closer together). One of the guards opened up some panels in the table, and then Jon was unceremoniously tossed directly under it face down, facing the center of the C-shaped couch. The guards then roughly manhandled him, placing an arm in one hole, then the other, then with the ankles, locking him into place. Jon didn't know much, but this was an awkward, humiliating position: his hands and his bare feet were sticking up from under the table, but underneath, he was helpless, suspended about two inches above the carpet. He knew why they would want his feet sticking out from under the table, but his hands? Must be a suspension thing. Either way, with his hands and feet above the table and the rest of his body below, Jon was completely helpless.

"Hey guys," Pat shouted, "I think it's time we put the Table to good use!"

"Capital idea!" J.C. shouted, which was some high language for someone who looked like a hippie burnout (then again, the Master was no better). People gathered around and sat on the couch, and given his perspective from under the table, all Jon could see is ... of course: people's legs and feet. Sitting right down directly in front of him were feet that Jon was far too familiar with, already: those of Pat. People to either side of him leaned over and placed drinks directly in Jon's above-table hands, each saying "Can you hold that for me, boy?" Jon, not having a choice, did so. Also, being suspended in such an awkward fashion was not making for the most comfortable position ever. Jon immediately regretted listening to that voice earlier.

Jon yelped at the immediate scraping of fingernails against his right sole. "Who the fuck was that?!" he uncharacteristically shouted. "Oh yes, Nate," Jon overheard the Master saying. "Keep that up. He loves it when his feet are tickled. Ryan, grab the other one, won't you?" Suddenly Jon felt a pair of fingernails on each foot scraping off tickles of him, and fuck did it tickle. His toes curled and flexed to try and get away but the two people that Jon couldn't see behind him were going to town on his bare soles, laughing in his adorable high pitch. Pat lifted his feet up and placed one on each cheek of Jon's face, holding it in position while it laughed.

"This is what you get for spilling wine, boy!" Pat said, patting him on the face with his left foot as he did so. That same foot then began moving up the side of Jon's face slowly, the toes running through Jon's hair while Jon did his best to ignore his own feet getting tickled. "You're enjoying this, aren't you boy?" Pat asked, imploringly. All Jon could do was cackle in response.

The tickling abruptly stopped. Jon could see the top of half of Pat leaning forward, so he must've directed the 'lers to stop their action. Pat now placed his feet firmly on the floor, directly below Jon's suspended face. There they were: large, a bit of hair, a bit of Jon's saliva shine still visible on them.

"Jon, do you like my feet?" Pat asked, casually.

Jon's despair was overwhelming. He really didn't like where this was going, but had to play the game. "Yes sir," he said, "I do."

"Well," Pat responded, "that's very nice of you. In fact, would you go as far as to say that you *love* my feet?"

Fuck Jon hated this. "Yes," he said in dry monotone, "I do."

"What's your favorite part of my feet, Jon?"

Jon's responded with whatever the first thing was that came to his mind. "Your toes sir. I really enjoy your long toes."

"Are they sexy toes?" Pat asked while curling them on the ground, slightly.

"Yes," Jon responded, "they're sexy toes."

"Well that's great Jon, 'cos I was hoping I can put a few of them in your mouth just to see if you can suck the flavor out of them. Would you like to do that, Jon?"

Given no one could see his face under the table, all Jon could do was simply mime out the word "fuck". The only way out is through ...

"Please," Jon lied, "I'd love nothing more."

Without a moment's hesitation, Pat slowly lifted his left foot up and started inching his hairy toes into Jon's mouth. He seemed to be bypassing the big toe altogether, focusing on all the other toes, fitting as many as he could into Jon's mouth so he could shrimp them. Jon simply closed his eyes as this happened, trying to think of other things as Pat slowly slid his toes in and out of Jon's mouth. "Can you fit all four of them in there?" Pat asked as he tried to maneuver his pinky toe in as well -- alas, it was not to be.

Pat pulled his foot out of Jon's mouth at which point Jon could feel the wine glasses in his hands being picked up almost simultaneously. "Do you like feet in general, Jon?" Pat asked, undoubtedly with a shit-eating grin if Jon could see it.

"Yes I do, sir," Jon answered mechanically.

"Well how about this then: why don't you suck on my other toes while the rest of your appendages get to feel up as many feet as they like."

Without even asking for a response from Jon, Pat raised up his right foot to Jon's mouth, slowly inserting all the toes but the big one (the big toe was somewhat up against Jon's nose, however, forcing him to inhale some of Pat's manly footscent). As this happened, Jon suddenly felt a pair of feet start to fondle his right foot ... then another on his left, then a pair in each hand. All of his exposed flesh was being fondled by male feet right now.

"Go on," Pat encouraged, "feel up the feet in your hands."

Jon, trying to block this all out, had his hand clumsily and lazily rub the feet that were touching each hand (the left one was a bit hairier while the right one had short, stub toes), all while the feet his own feet were getting an intense game of footsie going. What the fuck kind of invitational was this?

Meanwhile, Jon was fighting desperately to not think about the fact the tips of Pat's toes were trying to run along his teeth, touching Jon's gumline, somehow humiliating him even more than he was before. Jon's tongue touched Pat's toes only accidentally, but it was enough to leave a pungent flavor on his tastebuds. Feet in his hand, feet on his feet, feet in his mouth -- the next five minutes simply overloaded his brain with the word "feet" and nothing else.

At the end of Jon's podiacal mindfuck, the feet stopped rubbing his exposed flesh and Pat removed his foot from Jon's mouth, leaving a tangy aftertaste that registered as a hard negative for Jon. He realized that if Hell were a real thing, having to endure an experience with feet at the "Table" for eternity would probably be it. Pat's feet were at the floor, but his toes were wiggling, readjusting to not wearing Jon's mouth as a sock.

"Did you enjoy that, boy?" Pat asked, dripping with sarcasm.

"Yes I did," said Jon, full of hatred and bile.

Immediately some fingernails on Jon's exposed feet began scraping again, culling as many tickles as they could out of him, scratching the undersides of his toes in particular to great effect. The tickling was so sudden that the initial jolt caused Jon's body to jerk violently, shaking the glasses on the table for a moment. Even has Jon's body could only emit the weakest of cackles now, Pat continued playing with the footservant.

"Well Jon," he started, "now that you're under ticklish duress, I can think of no better time than to graciously ask you what you, Jon, really want. Do you want more tickles? Do you want me to wear your mouth as a sock again? Please, enlighten me Jon. What do you really want?"

Jon was cackling, as his feet felt like they were absolutely on fire, to which that voice that had been egging him on about everything caused him to scream at the top of his lungs "I WANT MY FEET TO BE WORSHIPED BY THE MASTER!"

The tickling immediately stopped. The room seemed to go silent, except for that faint classical music in the background. No one moved. In air was filled with an unspoken tension. Then, Jon heard a single sound: the slapping of a sandal against a bare heel as it walked. Over and over again, louder and louder it got, and then suddenly he saw a pair of flip-flopped feet walk into view, standing right in front of Pat, the Master's own toes inches from Jon's face.

"Really?" the Master said. "You want me to worship your feet?"

"All night," Jon lied.

Jon didn't see anything, but heard the two snaps again. He heard the marching of those bodyguards once again, coming closer to the Table. The master spoke directly to them: "He'll be exhausted and pass out. Toss him in my room and keep a man posted. I'll be in after the guests have left."

"Yes sir," one of them said in a flat monotone.

Guests around the table made a bit of room while the guards carefully extracted Jon from the table and carried him away. The second Jon was removed from the table, conversation in the room continued as normal. Held lightly in the guards arms' (because after that ordeal, what kind of energy would he have left in him anyways?), Jon instinctively rubbed his hands against his wrists, blessed to finally have movement again. The guards carried him up some grand staircases, all dimly lit as evening approached, and eventually they opened up a room with a double-door entrance. The lights weren't on, but Jon could clearly see a gigantic bed with fluffy white sheets taking up a great deal of space. The guards unceremoniously tossed (tossed!) Jon onto the fluffy bed, causing Jon to bounce once before landing, settling in soon thereafter. My goodness, Jon thought, this felt like a cloud. He wasn't sure if there was memory foam underneath or what, but for the first time in a long time, Jon felt instantaneously comfortable.

Two guards left the room and shut the double doors behind them. One guard stayed in, looking at Jon without any visible emotion on his face -- not like that mattered, of course, as Jon could feel his eyelids get heavy with exhaustion. Before long, he passed out completely.

+ + +

Jon awoke only because he could hear some muffled, audible sounds coming from the hallway. His eyelids half-opened while the rest of his body remained motionless. The night moon was illuminating the room Jon was in, coins of light splayed out across the bed. The voice from the hallway came even closer, and soon the door opened. All Jon could make out was the last sentence the Master was speaking:

"... yeah, and tell Pat he owes me now! Yeah yeah, alright, goodnight."

Jon stirred somewhat, slowly turning over, fighting every impulse he had to go to sleep again 'cos after his ordeal of the past few days, this bed felt like heaven.

"You want me to get the sack out?" the guard said to the Master.

"How was he while I was away?" asked the Master.

"Passed out. Boy be tired."

"Ya know," the Master started before going silent, contemplating. "Ya know, I think we'll be OK. The psychological profile showed him as being submissive, and I think he just *really* wants to have his feet worshiped, so it's OK: I'll be fine."

"Should I stand guard sir?" This guard was all business.

"Actually," the Master said, "why don't you stand out in the hallway. I'll enjoy it a lot more if there's no one around to hear anything. Quasi-privacy, let's say."

"You got it, boss." With that, the guard closed the bedroom doors behind him, leaving the Master and Jon together in a completely unlit room.

"Well," started the Master, addressing Jon as he made his way over to the adjoining bathroom, "I must say Jon, I'm impressed."

Jon was still rubbing his eyes, trying to wake himself up. "In what way?"

"Oh," the Master started, "just with your tenacity. The fact that it was less than a week ago when I purchased you and you've just been impressing me at every turn. Maybe it's fleeting thing, but I'm really, really fascinated by you, Jon."

"Me," Jon said coyly, "or my feet?"

The Master snickered. Jon heard some sort of rumbling of glass materials in the bathroom. "Let's go with both," the Master said. "Your feet are absolutely a feast for the eyes and, I must say, your go-get-'em personality is intriguing me as well."

The Master emerged from the bathroom with a large, beautifully made glass bong. The Master set it on a chest near the foot of the bed.

"Weed?" Jon asked.

"Only the world's best," the Master said, prepping the device, which Jon could now see was already filled with water. "C'mon Jon: take a hit."

"I'm ... that's really not my scene," Jon said, earnestly.

"It is is now," the Master shot back in a firm tone. Jon knew he was cornered. He got off the bed, walked over to where the chest was, and took the lighter that the Master handed to him. He lit the spout, burning through buds, and started breathing in, bubbling the water inside as smoke shot up his lungs. Jon held his breath, but started coughing violently right away.

"There's water in the bathroom," the Master directed. Jon ran over there and poured himself a glass quickly, soon gulping it on down to fight the embers inside of his throat. Residual coughs came back, but they started to slowly dissipate. As Jon braced the sink of this too-lavish bathroom, Jon could hear more smoke bubbles being formed, as the Master was taking a giant hit of his own. Jon shook his head and stared into the mirror: he looked like shit, worn down and dragged out. Jon put his fingers to the bags under his eyes, unsure if he wasn't getting enough sleep or if his body was simply near its breaking point. Either way, it--

"Get back in here, boy!" the Master shouted.

Jon had no choice. He went back into the bedroom and just flopped onto the bed, his bare feet habitually rubbing against each other a bit for warmth The Master also got on the bed, leaving the unshod young gentleman on their backs, staring up at the Master's relatively unadorned ceiling in the dark of the night.

"Don't worry," the Master said, "you won't feel high right now but in a few minutes this shit will kick in and blow your mind. It's ... some powerful stuff. Once it hits, I'm going to go to fucking town on you, you got it?"

"Yes sir," Jon said, reflexively. A few moments passed, the boys remaining motionless, staring at the great big nothing ahead of them.

"Can I ask you something?" Jon started.

"Sure thing," the Master said.

"How ... how did you get all of this?"

"Heh," the Master chortled, "by being a genius. Let's put it this way, Jon: when you invent a program that is soon to be used by every computer, smartphone, and electronic device that's ever made -- and you get a hefty per diem on every single device sold -- you don't have to worry about working another day in your life for as long as you live. At which point, with your amassed billions of dollars, you need to have fun. So what better way to make money and do what you truly love than by establishing a black market for tickle toys to be obtained and traded as you see fit. Every day is infinite heaven, Jon, and I wouldn't trade it for anything ever."

"Do you ever worry about getting caught?" Jon asked.

"Ha!" The Master exclaimed. "Hell no. Not when you have as much money as I do. When you have infinite wealth, you can pay to have a mole in every police department, every governmental bureau, every goddamn thing ever. I know four weeks ahead of time if anyone's even remotely suspicious of me. 'sides," he started, now turning over on his side to look at Jon in the face, "how can I hate a law that has been so beneficial to me?"

"I guess you're right," Jon said, still laying on his back. "Good thing Patrick Lund never got wind of you."

"You kidding me?" the Master said, a smile dripping from his words, "I was one of the guys who tickled him?"

Jon turned to face him. "Really?"

"Tao Kappa Lambda for life, baby. Those pledge weeks were what we became *known* for. Those were our reputations. Officially, I have to say that Patrick Lund should burn in tickle hell for what he did, but c'mon: I get to suck on the feet of a footservant or tickle him to orgasm anytime I want -- which is rather frequently."

Jon tried to turn over a sympathetic card: "But what if ... ya know, someone doesn't want to be taken? I mean, I don't think anyone wants to be here."

The Master's hand reached out and turned Jon's face towards his own. "I don't know how the Black Feather works Jon, but all I know is that they only abduct the people that have nothing left to give in their life."

Jon jerked his face back, a bit offended. "I had lots going on. I had a whole life in front of me."

"No," the Master sighed, "you didn't. I don't know all the details, but from what I gathered from the Black Feather, you had a dead-end job, a fairly placid relationship with some girl, and you were going to be fired in a month anyways. You had no extracurricular activities or hobbies of note -- Jon, the Black Feather saved you from a life of total uselessness. You should be thanking them."

Jon calmly marked his words: "So I get abducted but you hail Patrick Lund up as your savior?"

The Master laughed. "Dear goodness no. He's in the basement, Jon. He's in my basement, with the machines."

Jon's eyes were briefly filled with terror: "He's here?"

"Has been for a year now, Jon. What do you think the climax of the party was? I brought over rich, powerful figures from numerous industries that share my exact same interests. While you were sleeping here, we went down to visit him from behind a glass wall, and watched him cry and plead as the machines tickled his feet and extracted his 2000th consecutive load of hot sticky cum. I don't like seeing people in misery as a general rule, but I like seeing him as my toy, and I like him seeing me watch him, knowing full well that it was me that put him there."

At this moment, Jon's brain warped, his vision feeling like that film effect where they zoom in while they roll the camera back. The back of his brain felt like it kept on hitting "levels", each one leading him to a goofier level of base stupidity. Jon's fears about this conversation melted away, and only one thought crossed his mind, which he spoke out loud: "Fuck, I'm stoned man."

The Master started giggling. "Yeah, it just hit me too. Oh *man!* Dude. I'm ... fuck, I'm gone."

Jon started laughing a bit, "Yeah, me too."

The Master suddenly stood up and wobbled over to Jon's side of the bed, placing himself near Jon's feet. "Now Jon," he said, grinning like a moron, "have you ever been stoned before?"

"I mean," Jon fumbled for words, "yeah, I mean, like, a while ago, yes. Not recently, but yes."

"OK," the Master said, "and have you ever had your toes sucked on while stoned?"

Jon grinned against his best will. "No ..."

"Well then," the Master said, reeling his face around to the underside of Jon's feet. Jon could feel him take a great big inhalation, his body shuddering with pleasure as it did so. The Master's tongue outstretched and licked a small patch of skin on Jon's arch. Jon giggled and reflexively pulled his foot away.

"Hehe, stop that!" he mustered out.

"Oh Jon," the Master said, "I'm only just getting started." The Master slowly enveloped Jon's toes with his warm mouth, and Jon let out a gasp: what an astonishingly erotic gesture. To feel that tongue slowly envelop the tips of his toes with such a moist orifice, it was surprisingly sensual. Jon's hands gripped the bedsheets he was on as the Master's tongue simply slithered around, slurping up the spaces in-between Jon's toes, covering every square inch of Jon's foot with horny, wet saliva. The Master proceeded to slowly drag his teeth down Jon's instep, tickling him, lifting up Jon's right foot so that the Master could playfully gnaw on his heels slightly. Jon, against his better nature, was feeling somewhat horny by the experience. The Master then went after Jon's other foot, licking it, dragging his tongue of the tops of Jon's feet, plastering the sides with saliva. Especially when stoned out of his gourd, Jon couldn't help but admit that the oversensitized feeling of a mouth on his toes was nothing short of overwhelming.

As the Master laid there, sucking out every possible molecule of taste as he could from Jon's left foot, Jon, somewhat instinctively, took his right foot and ran his toes through the Master's hair, slowly. The Master moaned with approval. Jon slid his right foot then slowly across the Master's cheek, causing the Master to shift his oral attention to that foot. With the left appendage now free, Jon now stroked the Master's hair and cheek with that foot as well. Before long, that little voice inside Jon's head took over:

"You like this, don't you, boy?" he said.

'Fuck," the Master said, "yes I fucking do. This is so fucking hot."

"You fucking *love* my feet, don't you?"

The Master could only speak between toeslurps: "God yes. More than anything ever."

"You'd do anything for my sexy toes, right?"

"Yes!" the Master exclaimed, head-over-heels in lust.

"Have you ever had a footjob before?" Jon intoned.

The Master stopped his slurping and looked up directly at Jon. "Are you serious?"

"Does it look like I'm serious?" Jon said with a stoic face.

The Master's smile was gigantic. Jon was certain that the Master had never been happier in his life. The Master knelt on the bed, eager as a puppy: "So what do we do?" he asked.

Jon seized the situation: "Well, there are a few things. For one, you have a way to monitor the other prisoners, right?"

"Yes," the Master said eagerly. "I have a laptop that gives me control of the entire facility."

"Bring that out," Jon ordered. The Master got up and proceeded to open up some drawers. "Oh," Jon continued, "is there also some restraints we could use?"

The Master turned to Jon, giving a delightful, pleasured smile. "Yes. They're already attached to the posts of the bed. They're on a auto-retractable string. You see them?"

Jon looked and saw these loose, soft rubber loops attached to strings, looking like oversized rubber bands. "Yes, I got them."

"Sweet," the Master said, soon bringing over a laptop to the bed. Jon went over to look at it, and saw it was very high-tech, the screen filled with about eight different windows of video monitoring. Some slaves were being worked over by their keepers. Some were awake and doing nothing in their cells, their feet sticking out into that hallway from earlier. There was another window that seemed to have thumbnails of dozens upon dozens more.

"Where's Jose?" Jon asked.

"Computer," the Master said, the computer responding with a light tone of recognition, "show footslave Jose."

Without touching the keyboard, a screen popped up of Jose in a room with appeared to be Jason, Jose suspended by chains just as Jon was before, Jason digging into Jose's pits and Jose clearly losing his mind.

"What do you need this for?" the Master asked.

"Well," Jon said, "I'm going to overwhelm your senses. You're going to be stoned, tied up, receiving a footjob while watching video feeds of your slaves being worked over. How is that not absolute heaven?"

"That," the Master stammered. "That sounds amazing. What now?"

Jon, still a bit intoxicated, was a bit amazed by how easy it was to take control of the situation. Somehow that little voice in his head knew that despite the multimillion dollar empire, the Master was still a submissive at heart, and Jon was finding his new role surprisingly easy to adept to. He looked directly at the Master's face, eager.

"Strip down to your undies," Jon ordered. The Master did so instantaneously, as if thinking the speediness of it would please his new dom. He stood there, purple boxers hiding a raging boner in the boy's pants, totally exposed. Jon looked at the messy-haired young man, his face covered by neither hat nor glasses -- this was just a kid. A twenty-something kid with an uncontrollable passion and way too much money. He had probably never been dominated in his entire life, and for whatever reason, it wasn't something he could buy safely.

"Should I get on the bed now?" the Master said, already starting to move in that direction.

"No," Jon said. "You're going to take another bong hit first."

The Master's eyes opened up wide. "But sir," he said, "that would make me, like, super-stoned."

Jon leaned over and whispered in the Master's ear, "I know."

The Master grinned, proceeded to go over to the bong still on the chest at the foot of the bed. He looked up at Jon. "Are you going to partake as well?"

"No," Jon said, "I need a clear mind to dominate a footbitch such as you."

The Master really liked being called a bitch, apparently. He smiled and then took a massive, massive bong hit. Even Jon, still pretty high, thought it was a bit much. The Master released, and had no coughs. He was an experienced smoker, apparently.

"OK," Jon said, "now get on the bed."

"Hold on a second," the Master said, "I gotta ... I gotta let this work through me a bit."

"Hey," Jon shouted, "do you want my toes feeling up your dick or not?"

The Master's eyes widened. "Yes sir." He jumped on the center of the bed, almost knocking the laptop off in the process. Jon told him to sit tight while he pulled the giant rubber band restraints from each post of the bed, wrapping them around the Master's appendages, each one pulling him into a taught spread-eagle formation. The process took a few minutes, and by the time he was done, the Master pushed his head back as far as he could into the pillow, saying "Holy *shit!* Jon, I'm ... fuck. Just ... fuck."

"Good boy," Jon said. "Now before we begin, where's a good pad of paper to write on?"

The Master's breaths were short, somewhat eroticized. "Bottom drawer of the credenza. Same one where I pulled out -- fuck -- pulled out the laptop."

Jon opened it up, saw a pad of paper and a few other things there. Jon smirked. He opened up the drawer to the right of that one as well, and saw it filled with used, dirty white ankle socks and sweatblackened flip-flops: the Master's own personal drawer of jackoff toys. Jon, with pad and paper in hand, saw the socks as well as a few other things from the laptop drawer, had some ideas.

"Will," he said to the Master, using the formal name he overheard at the party, "what is the voice command on your computer for overhead announcements?"

"Overhead," the Master said. "Why do you need to know?"

"Never you mind," Jon said, "just enjoy while I write something out." Jon tossed a pair of worn ankle socks onto the Master's face, and the Master immediately inhaled, his cock violently twitching in approval under those boxers. The twitched happen more and more as Jon finished writing out something.

When done, Jon got up on the bed and turned the laptop towards the Master's face so he could see the live stream of Jose getting the daylights tickled out of him. Jon sat on the Master's stomach facing him, largely so he didn't even have to look at the Master's quivering erection. Jon removed the ankle socks and slapped both of his bare feet on the Master's face, covering it completely.

"Inhale, bitch," he said. The Master did, and soon Jon could feel some involuntary bucking from the Master's hips -- boy did he enjoy this. "You like that, Will?"

The Master's head turned left and right, helpless, "*Fuck, more than anything in the universe!*"

"Have you ever been this horny in your life?"

"No!" he shouted.

"Do you want to lick the soles of my bare, sexy feet until you cum?"

"YES!" the Master shouted again. Jon looked back at the door, fearing the Master was being loud enough to alert the guards. Nothing.

"OK," Jon said. "You're not in much of a position to talk, so in order for you to get everything you've ever wanted, you have to read three things for me. I've written them out on this pad. If you can say them perfectly out loud, then you will get your wish. Sound like a deal?"

The Master's head nodded violently. "Yes yes yes yes! Please yes!"

"Good," Jon said, whipping out the pad of paper. He held up a page in front of the Master's face. "Now read it."

The Master did so, slowly: "I, the Master, love male feet more than anything in the world. They make me so fucking horny, and all I want is to jerk myself stupid onto some manly toes." The Master then pressed his head far back into the pillow again. "Fuck, this is so goddamn hot!"

"I know," said Jon. Now let's go to page two, shall we? I must warn you -- this one's a bit longer."

Jon held up the paper, which the Master read out loud like a rote mechanism: "Computer. Overhead." Jon heard the computer's recognition tone. "This is the Master speaking. I've had such a good time today that I've had a change of heart." Jon stroked the side of the Master's face with his right foot as he did so to keep his mind where he wanted it. "Effective immediately, all prisoners are to be released, as well as all footservants. Guards, please release them and make the necessary arrangements to return them to their respective homes. The only exception is footservant Aaron. All keepers are hereby ordered to work over Aaron until further notice." Even with Jon stroking his face with his toes, the Master leaned up and whispered to Jon: "Dude, this is really long."

"We're almost there, I promise," Jon whispered back, tapping on the page again.

The Master continued reading: "Once all procurements are off the premises, guards can go home until further notice." The page was done. "Dude," the Master said, "did I just ..."

Jon immediately shoved the toes of his right foot into the Master's mouth. "Suck, boy. That was a long one." The Master's toes greedily swirled around Jon's toes, tickling him, and after a minute, Jon pulled his foot out. He turned to the third page. Jon tapped on it again: "One more."

The Master read: "I hereby declare myself to be Jon's personal foot bitch from now to eternity." The Master closed his eyes, content. He then looked at Jon in stoned earnest: "Really? I get to do that?"

Jon dismounted from the bed, grabbing something from the drawer below. "Yes, but not now," he warned. "Absence makes the heart grow fonder, and you're not getting my feet until you prove to me that you really, really want them." Jon had grabbed an armful of socks and sandals and he placed them on the bed, soon placing them all on the Master's face, shoving some of the socks into his mouth. All the Master could do was just muffle some words. Before long, Jon couldn't even see the Master's face, as it was covered in male footwear. Jon noticed the Master's cock, and precum had positively soaked the front of the Master's boxers. Jon found a pair of scissors in the one of the drawers and quickly cut off the Master's undies, letting the Master's massive cock spring forth, engorged with blood, swelling with horny thoughts. Jon reached for something else from under the drawer, and began speaking to the Master directly: "Now, Will, you're going to get what you really want. Too much of it even. I'm going to take a guess that you've never experienced some of your own devices, but this one, well, it'll drive you bonkers." With that, Jon attached the small two-ringed jacking device that he experienced oh so long ago to the Master's cock. It was a tough fit given how swollen with horniness it was, but Jon managed to do so, and then flicked the switch. The ring at the cock rim and the one at the base came together a bit, then parted, then came together, then parted, pumping all along. The Master's body started spazzing out, twitching and convulsing against his will. Jon couldn't see the Master's face under the pile of smelly socks and sandals, but could hear the Master try to muffle something.

"And with that," Jon said, "goodbye."

Jon opened the big doors to the bedroom and closed them behind him, hearing a muffled scream of agony shortly before the door latched shut. Off in the distance, he saw one of the guards from earlier. Jon called him over. The guard walked up to Jon, suspicious.

"Shouldn't you be back with the Master?" he asked.

"He's done," Jon said, "and sleeping like a baby. I wouldn't disturb him if I were you. Now as for whatever that announcement was, how do you get me home?"

The guard looked up at the double bedroom doors before Jon snapped his fingers in his face. "Hey buddy, " he said, "get me out of here. Master's orders."

The guard was clearly conflicted, but Jon's confidence in the matter -- added to the fact that he didn't seem scared or lying or have the urge to run -- lead the guard to believe he was telling the truth. "Come with me, sir," the guard said, leading him downstairs into the main guest room where the party was held only hours ago. Jon didn't see much as he was lead outside the premises, but as he passed by the double doors leading into the kitchen, he caught a glimpse of Aaron being surrounded by guards. Jon smiled a bit, walking on that fucking ticklish rug for the last time time.

As Jon was being transported home some several hours later (and mercifully given a pair of flip-flops at some point so he wouldn't be barefoot outside), Jon was feeling nervous, fearing that at any point, a guard or a TSA agent or someone would stop him, Jon's masterful escape plan having been found out once and for all. However, that didn't happen, and some 24 hours after closing that bedroom door, Jon found himself home at long last. In many ways, he didn't believe it, but his sigh of relief upon seeing the front door to his apartment was almost too much for him; he had never been more happy to be home. Even now, Jon's feet still tingled a bit as they took each step, but Jon knew exactly who to thank for starting the chain of events that caused that ...

+ + +

Tommy was in his apartment, late on a Friday night, drinking a beer while watching some fetish porn on his computer. In all honesty, as hard as he tried to jerk himself off at night, he just couldn't do it, not since Jon inexplicably left. While Tommy did hear that Jon had apparently been afflicted with some sort of foreign virus while away, he knew the truth, having seen him and countless other young men being sold to auction for private tickle collectors. The idea, in its own way, was kind of hot, but the guilt that Tommy's actions lead to having Jon get kidnapped and sold into erotic slavery was too much -- Tommy would be lying to himself he didn't note that had spent a few nights crying over it, racked with guilt, sending him into a spiraling depression.

As another swig of beer finished swirling down Tommy's throat, he went to the restroom to relieve himself, shaking his head as thoughts continued torturing his brain. He flushed the toilet, washed his hands, and dried them on his towel before going back to his computer. The second he opened the door, however, he saw that someone was sitting there in his computer chair. Tommy stood there for a moment, blankly staring, trying to register what was happening, and then as soon as the figure spoke, he knew what was going on:

"Hello, Tommy."

Tommy's eyes went wide. "Jon? *Jon?*"

"Yes," Jon replied, calmly.

"Holy fuck!" Tommy exclaimed. "Jon, you're here! You're back! That's ... how did you get out? I ..." Suddenly the gravity of the situation dawned on him. Tommy fell to his knees and looked right at Jon, wearing jeans, a t-shirt, and a new pair of flip-flops. "Jon, I'm so sorry. I had no idea. I thought it was --"

Jon lifted up his sandaled foot and pressed it right onto Tommy's mouth, quieting him.

"You listen here and you listen good," Jon said to his terrified co-worker, "I don't know what exactly happened, but guess what Tommy? They almost took my entire life away from me -- all because of you. Because of your selfish actions. Because of your uncontainable foot fetish. So guess what now, boy?"

Tommy slurred out a word even with the bottom of Jon's sandal pressed directly on his lips: "What?"

"You're mine." Tommy's eyes were struck with terror, Jon's tone definitive, unrelenting. "Your life is mine. Just as you almost ruined mine, I get to completely run yours, and you're going to let me, because you have a male foot fetish and you're in love with my feet. So consider this Lesson One, Day One. Your first task is simple: agree to me fucking you over like you did me by kissing the tops of my toes."

Jon placed his feet on the floor as Tommy was on all fours. Tommy's head tilted down, looking at Jon's perfect feet staring at him from those sexy sandals. He looked up again and saw Jon's face was stern, dead-on serious, and Tommy knew the only way he could ever possibly relieve his guilt was by agreeing to whatever Jon had in mind for him over the course of the next ... however long.

With his heart absolutely pounding with both lust and terror, Tommy's head tilted forward again, staring directly at the feet he so craved. Tommy closed his eyes, leaned in, and kissed the tops of Jon's sexy raw toes.

Tommy enjoyed the taste, but, as he would find out over the coming years, had absolutely no idea what kind of humiliation he was in for over the rest of his life ...

ABOUT THE AUTHOR

James T. Medak is a celebrated erotica author living in Chicago, having previously written How to Be a Tickle Slave *(which was hailed as an "instant classic" by the Big Tickle Blog) and* My, What Ticklish Feet You Have. *Medak has appeared at various tickle events in Chicago, and can be followed on Twitter @JamesTMedak*

4127663R00095

Printed in Great Britain
by Amazon.co.uk, Ltd.,
Marston Gate.